GOOD GIRL

JANA ASTON

Edited by RJ Locksley

Cover Design by Letitia Hasser
Cover Photo by Wander Aguiar
Cover Model Thiago Lusardi

Interior Design by Erik Gevers

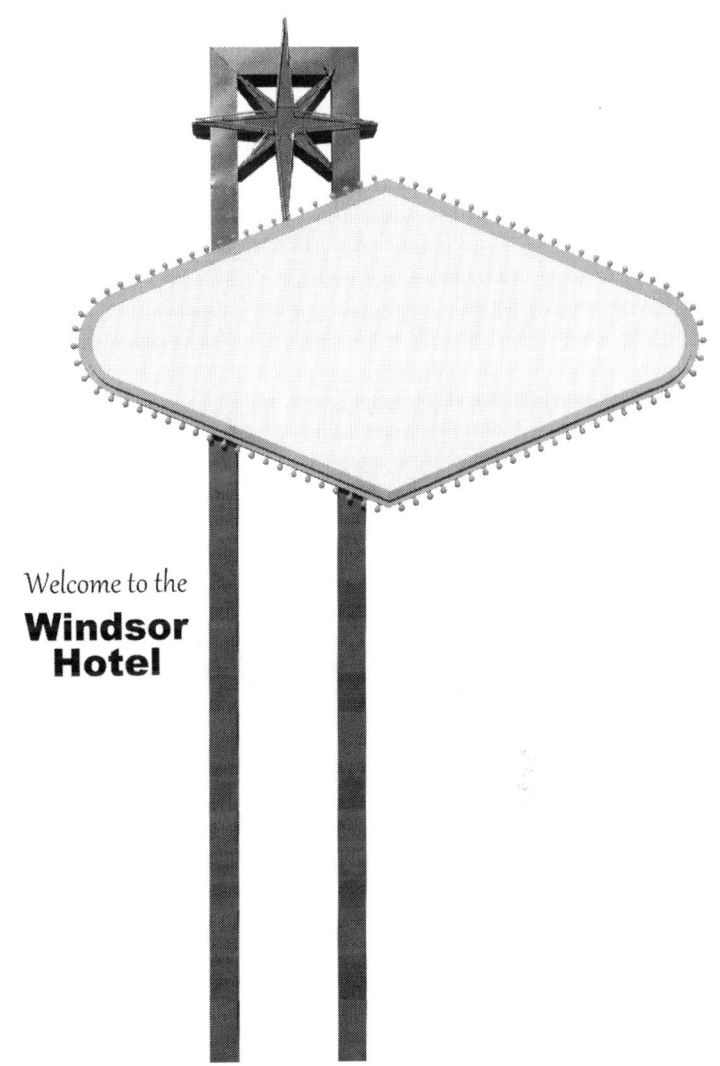

Welcome to the
**Windsor
Hotel**

GOOD GIRL

Jana Aston

New York Times Bestselling Author

ONE

LYDIA

"WE'RE NOT LEAVING this bar until you kiss someone." Payton says this as if we were in the midst of having a conversation about me kissing someone. We weren't. I nod all the same because we're best friends and I'm used to this kind of outburst from her.

"So you want me to kiss someone and then we can leave?" I set my glass down on the bar top and twist a bit in my seat as if I'm scanning the room for options. I'm not, not really, but I'm happy to play along.

"Yeah. Once you've at least kissed someone we can leave."

"At least kissed?" I turn back to her with a laugh. "How far do you want me to go? In a bar? With a stranger?" I'm laughing because this conversation is ridiculous—and yet... the idea of it entices me. The idea that I could have my pick of any man in this bar and ask him to kiss me. Or maybe even feel me up in the hallway. Maybe he'd take charge and press me against the wall. Shove his knee between my thighs while he ran kisses down my jaw before covering my

1

lips with his own.

Yeah, that was oddly specific.

I tuck a strand of hair behind my ear and let my eyes stray past Payton to the two men sitting on the other side of her. I've been discreetly eyeing them all night. One of them has a British accent. He's drunk and obsessing about a woman he just broke up with. Or who broke up with him—I'm not sure and I don't really care. The object of my desire is guy number two.

Guy number two is perfect.

He's so perfect I can't even look directly at him, hence the discreet glances. He's totally out of my league. Dark tousled hair with a hint of a wave. Perfectly cut, and I just know it would be soft under my fingers and not full of gross hair product. He's got facial hair, trimmed close as if he can't commit between a stubble and a beard, and the darkest brown eyes that make my stomach drop when they catch mine. His forearms are tanned and lined with sinewy muscle. They will be the focus of my fantasies for at least the next month.

He rubs the pad of his thumb against the pad of his index finger as his friend talks, but not in an anxious way. Slowly, as if it's something he does when he thinks, or perhaps it's a thing he does while he listens. His nails are short and nicely shaped. I'd guess based on his hands that he works at a desk, but based on what I can see of his body, his hobby is the gym.

His forefinger takes another slow drag across his thumb and oh, holy Jesus, I am imagining something else entirely right now.

I need to get laid.

"You need to get laid," Payton says at the exact moment the man's gaze rises from the bar top to my eyes. I die about ten thousand times, but Payton is unaware that I've just died so she continues babbling about finding someone for me to kiss before we can leave. Mister Perfect's eyes are still on mine.

"I'll do it," he says.

Oh, my God. Wait, is he talking to me? Is this happening? Surely I misheard. Misunderstood. He's talking to someone behind me or the bartender or the drunk British guy. I take a quick look over my shoulder to see who's behind me. There's no one behind me.

"I'll do it," he repeats and for a heartbeat my brain short-circuits. Firm yes, is what I'm thinking. Firm yes. Where will we do it? I don't want to do it here, that would be weird. I don't think we should go back to his place, he's a total stranger. He could come to my place. Yes. Payton could run to Target or something and give us privacy. I wonder if he'll mind that I only have a single bed? I knew I should have bought a bigger one but it was more money and my room is tiny and I needed room for my sewing machine. Holy shit, this is happening. This man who is too hot to look directly at wants to have sex with me. I blink and then he finishes speaking, a small smirk on his face. "I'll kiss you."

Oh.

Right. It's not like he'd be so taken with me—a random girl in a bar—he'd want to have sex with me based on nothing more than hearing my friend say I need to get laid. Dumb. I'm such an idiot. As if.

"She accepts," Payton says and she shoves me off my stool. For real, she actually gives me a little shove, similar to how I imagine mothers shove their children out the front door on the first day of school.

The man turns on his stool and I watch him take me in now that I'm standing. His eyes trail slowly up my bare legs and I want to kill Payton for dragging me into this bar. We just spent the weekend moving into our new apartment and I thought we were going out for a burger, so I'm in denim cutoffs and a tank top. I should have known better. Once we'd left the apartment Payton insisted we needed to check out the local action and here I am in cutoff shorts with my knobby knees watching a man who looks like he runs the world give me the once-over.

I bend one knee and tap my toes against the floor while I wonder if he's changing his mind, but then he stands. I assume he's going to close the distance between us and kiss me right there in front of everyone, but he doesn't. Instead he pauses in front of me. I have to tilt my head back to meet his eyes because he's about a foot taller than me. At best, the top of my head reaches his shoulders.

He's wearing jeans and loafers with that shirt that's rolled back to his elbows. I suspect his shoes cost more than anything I own. Honestly, that probably goes for his pants and shirt too. I'm fighting the urge to shove my hands into my back pockets and squirm under his gaze when he speaks.

"What's your name?"

"Lydia."

"Lydia," he repeats, his eyes on mine. Hearing him say my name must be some kind of foreplay for me because my heart is about to beat out of my chest. His voice is low and smooth, commanding and sexy as hell. "Not here," he states and takes my hand in his.

His hand is warm wrapped around mine and the simple physical contact sends goosebumps across my skin. Then he's moving, my hand in his as he guides us past the bar. "Brady, I'm using your office for a minute," he calls out to someone behind the bar. He doesn't so much as pause for a response, and a moment later we're alone.

The first thing I notice is that the office is nicer than I'd have expected for a bar. A large desk is before me, its surface tidy with a closed laptop atop it and a single pen lying beside it. A leather chesterfield sofa sits along the wall with an expensive but well-worn-in vibe.

The second thing I notice is the quiet. I hadn't thought it excessively loud in the bar, but from behind a closed door I realize how quiet it is without the clink of ice and the thumps of bottles. With only our breathing and my heartbeat echoing in my ears.

That is all the time I have for observation because he's turned to face me and he's tilted my chin up with his fingertip. Okay, one more observation. He smells amazing. He smells like someone I want to lie on top of, with my head tucked against his chest while he winds strands of my hair around his fingers. I know that's technically not a smell, but trust me on this. He smells like clean laundry and spice and virility. I want to climb all over him.

His eyes are hooded, his gaze moving from my eyes to my lips and back again with an unhurried confidence. I don't realize I'm holding my breath until he reminds me to breathe. His expression is a combination of aroused and amused.

I take a breath and wet my lips with my tongue. I

resist bouncing on my toes, but barely. There's a hint of a smile on his lips as he cups my jaw with one hand, the other coming to rest on my waist. His hand is so warm through the thin layer of my tank top, it almost feels like he's touching me directly. Then he bends his head to mine and kisses me.

Softly.

The hand at my waist stays where it is. The pressure of his fingers is firm, safe. An unnecessary but much-liked anchor because I'm not going anywhere. I place my palms on his chest, thrilling in the feel of the fabric pressed against my fingertips. Of the firmness of his body, the muscle and heat.

His lips leave mine, but only far enough for him to tilt his head a fraction before pressing them to my own again. His thumb sweeps across my cheek and I hum or moan in response, I'm not sure which, but I'm rewarded with another soft kiss as his lips coax mine apart. His facial hair feels stubbly against my skin and it only turns me on more. The light scratch against my own skin focuses my attention on his lips, on his strength, on the potency of his effect on me. He nips my bottom lip between his teeth and then he kisses me again, the pressure firmer, our tongues meeting, my knees weakening and my heart racing.

When he pulls back he has to steady me on my feet because I've leaned so far into him I'd have toppled over without the support. I feel breathless, like I've just run around the building. Minus a swipe of his thumb across his lower lip, he looks unaffected. He steps back and does another slow perusal of me from head to toe and I wonder what he sees. Does he see a woman he's attracted to? Or a girl he kissed as a favor? He looks a hundred times more pulled together than I feel.

"You've had your kiss. You can go home now, good girl."

TWO

LYDIA

THE WEEKEND PASSES in a flurry of breaking down cardboard boxes from our move and carting them out to the recycle bin at our apartment complex. Trips to Target for miscellaneous supplies and WinCo for groceries. Discovering Del Taco for the first time and trying just about everything from their buck-and-under menu. All while I replay that kiss in my mind over and over and over again.

Tomorrow I start my first job. Well, not my first job, of course. I've had jobs, lots of them. Summer jobs, after-school jobs, part-time jobs.

But tomorrow is my first post-graduation, full-time job. It's kind of a big deal, right? A rite of passage, the first day of my adult life.

I'm as surprised as anyone that it's in Las Vegas.

At a casino.

But it turns out that casinos have a ton of jobs, especially brand-new luxury casinos that haven't even opened yet. The Windsor will employ five thousand people by the time the doors open later this month, and I'm one of them.

I majored in human resources because I'm a helper. I love to help people. Payton likes to help people too, but she majored in marketing because there's no degree in party planning at LSU. Her words, not mine. She likes to help people have a good time, whereas I like to help people with things like making sure their taxes are paid on time. Growing up, I was the kind of kid who filled in every line on the Girl Trooper cookie order form and placed the x securely in the middle of the column so there was absolutely no confusion between an order for a Chocolate Chip versus a Grasshopper Mint. So I was super fun, obviously.

I didn't meet Payton until college, but she once told me she got kicked out of Girl Troopers. Something about a pyramid scheme for badges. I never got the full story because I accidentally admitted that I had stayed in Girl Troopers until the end of high school and she laughed so hard she crossed her legs and then toppled over.

I try to keep that tidbit to myself now. I mean, it wasn't something I ever voluntarily shared, it just sorta slipped out when she mentioned something about Girl Troopers one time. And the Girl Troopers filled a maternal void for me, growing up without another woman in the house. But whatever, I rocked Girl Troopers. I sold thirty-six hundred boxes of cookies my last year.

Don't worry, I most definitely keep that fact to myself.

The point is, I like to follow rules. I like dotting i's and crossing t's, so human resources is a perfect fit for me. I did internships in human resources the last two summers so I'm not totally new to this. And it's an entry-level job, of course, but I'm thrilled to be employed in my chosen field.

When the idea of moving to Las Vegas came up, I think Payton envisioned us living in a high-rise on the Strip, but I managed to convince her that Strip living isn't exactly realistic for two girls with about a decade each of student loans to pay off, so we're in Henderson. Also known as the suburbs. Our apartment is great. We have a gym and a pool and a dog park and bocce ball courts. I don't have a dog and I don't know anyone who plays bocce ball, or even what it is really, but it's nice to have. The leasing agent was really excited about it when we toured this place. Plus, Del Taco is so close I could walk there if I wanted to. I probably don't want to when it's a hundred degrees outside, but maybe in the fall. Most importantly, it's about a twenty-minute drive to work and by sharing a two-bedroom apartment, it's affordable.

Payton will be working at the Windsor as well since we were both lucky enough to land jobs during a job fair held on campus during our senior year. I grew up in one Bible Belt state, Tennessee, and went to school in another, Louisiana, so I never imagined myself moving to the center of sin, but here I am. And so far, it's just like anyplace else. Normal, really. Nice. Plus, there's no state income tax in Nevada so I can work on repaying my giant student loans back that much faster. Win-win.

My mind drifts to Friday night. To the bar. To that guy.

Good girl.

Why did it turn me on so much when that guy called me a good girl? That guy. That's how I have to remember the most attractive man I've ever kissed, or likely will ever kiss, because I never got his name.

Smooth, huh? The normal, polite time to have gotten that information would have been when he asked me for mine. But did I? No. I was too distracted by the idea that he was going to kiss me to think to ask for his name.

That's selfish, right? I was so focused on getting his lips on mine that I didn't even ask his name. Not that it matters. He kissed the hell out of me and sent me on my way, didn't he? His parting words echo in my mind over and over again. *You can go home now, good girl.* It was a condescending thing to say, but his tone wasn't patronizing. It was gruff. Low. Husky. Sexy as hell.

I'm sick of being good. The only kind of good I'm interested in being with that man is on my knees, with my lips wrapped around his dick while he tells me how good I am. *Good girl,* he'd whisper, and I'd like it. At least I like it in my imagination. I like it a lot. There's something very appealing about being called good when you're being very, very bad. Or when you're thinking of being bad, in my case.

I must be the sluttiest non-slut in the country. I'm a wannabe slut, which is just sorta sad, isn't it?

I spent my college years expecting to fall in love with the perfect guy. No, that's a lie. I'm not delusional, there's no such thing as a perfect guy. I know that, I do. But I expected to fall in love with someone worth it. Worth giving my virginity to. What? Surely you didn't think I put out in high school. I was very busy in high school, with the cookies and all. I don't want to brag or anything, but those cookies earned me a trip to Costa Rica. Granted, it was two weeks working on service projects so it wasn't like a beach trip or anything, but still.

In any case, I wasn't that interested in boys in high school. I know for lots of kids high school was about pushing boundaries and sneaking out to parties, but I had no interest. Parties sounded dangerous to me. Bad things happened at parties. Like socializing. Or underage drinking. Both scary. Good things happen when you study and work hard and volunteer your time to help others.

Graduating from college a virgin was not in my plans. Not even close. My goody-two-shoes-ness only goes so far. I fully expected I'd have earned the achievement badge for losing my virginity by the time graduation rolled around.

I envisioned myself as the kind of girl who married her college boyfriend, a wedding two months after graduation.

But it didn't happen.

I did not imagine myself as the kind of girl who'd be turned on by a stranger in a bar. Not ever. But that man, he's awoken something in me. Lust, I suppose. It wasn't just the kiss, it was him. The truth is I was eyeing him all night, my imagination rampant with the things he could do to me. The things I wanted him to do to me.

Like I said, wannabe slut. Who sits around imagining a strange man in a bar defiling her?

———

ON MONDAY MORNING I pull into the parking garage at the Windsor, my stomach full of excited butterflies about my first day of work. Payton is driving separately because she's in a different orientation group and we weren't sure if we'd be finishing at the same time or not.

So I'm on my own, just like a real grown-up, which I am. I'm an adult. I smile so hard I have to bite the inside of my cheek to control it. Not that it's necessary, I'm alone in my car so no one can see me grinning like an idiot.

I tap my fingertips against the steering wheel as I follow the signs pointing me to the employee parking sections of the garage. The resort opens in less than a month, and new hires will be starting en masse over the next four weeks. I'm a back-of-house hire, meaning I'm not on the front lines with the guests. I'll disappear into the corporate section of the resort that you never think about. Human resources, legal, marketing, IT, accounting: it's all in-house, tucked away out of sight.

Finding an open spot, I park and double-check my lipstick in the visor mirror, then I lock my car and make a mental note of where I've parked so I can find my car after work.

Okay, this is it. First day, here I come. It occurs to me that this is going to be a big year of firsts for me. First grown-up apartment. First job. First student loan payment.

And I'm absolutely, positively ditching my virginity before this year is over, so that'll be a great big first to check off my life list.

It's not as if I haven't had chances to ditch it prior to now, it's just that I haven't been that interested. I grew up with liberal parents in a conservative town, and I was sort of caught in the middle between those two worlds. Also, I simply wasn't in a huge hurry about it. Junior year I dated a guy I didn't like that much for way longer than I should have because I liked his cat. And no, that is not a euphemism for something cooler. It was an actual cat. A huge, black, long-haired cat with white mitten paws that went by the name of Mr. McGee, and I loved him.

The guy, not so much.

I'm not saying that it was either reasonable or logical, but it is what it is.

I was still waiting for something, you know? Something that made me feel like ripping my panties off, and that feeling never came. But whatever, this is my panty-ripping year. Or maybe it's my panty-dropping year? I probably won't rip my own panties off, will I? No, that would be weird. I'll drop them, for sure. I'm open to a guy ripping them off for me, but I've never worn the kind of underwear that would snap apart under a man's hands.

Shoot. I need new underwear.

If this is my year, I'm going to need the appropriate underwear for when it happens. I make a mental note to reward myself with new undies when I get my first paycheck. Another first! My first adult paycheck! Whoohoo!

I enter the building through the employee entrance, confident that I'm about to embark on the best year of my life.

An hour later, I'm certain of it.

THREE

I SPOT HIM WHILE I'm on the resort tour. That guy. The one from the other night who kissed me but whose name I did not get. He's just as perfect as I remembered. He makes my heart race and my pulse beat even faster than I remembered. Holy shit, I think he might work here. Which basically means I'm going to sleep with him, right? Right. It's totally happening. Meant to be. Kismet. Fate.

If he's interested, that is. But he did kiss me, so he might be interested in having sex with me. I think. I'm not exactly sure how that works for men. I've kissed men I didn't want to sleep with, obviously, but I think men are less picky than women. Aren't they? God, I hope he's less picky than I am, 'cause I think he's the one.

The one I'd like to have sex with, not *the one* one. No, of course not. I'm not so crazy that I'm planning marriage and babies with some man I do not know based on one perfect kiss. I still want to fall in love with the perfect man, whoever he is, and live happily ever after with him. It's just that I don't know when he's coming, that guy. What if I'm thirty before he shows up? I shouldn't have to wait until I'm thirty to

17

experience sex.

So no, I'm not planning on marrying him. I just want to give him my virginity, because I do think that he'd be really good at deflowering me based on that one perfect kiss. Because I feel something when I see him. Something I'm not that familiar with but that I'd classify as unbridled lust. A longing. A stirring, if you will.

Deflowering. What a ridiculous word. I make a mental note not to use it when I ask him to have sex with me.

"I think I saw that guy," I tell Payton when I see her in the employee cafeteria at lunch. By cafeteria I mean the swankiest cafeteria I've ever been in. There's a salad bar, a sandwich station, a pizza station and a variety of hot selections that look like they might change daily, based on the printed menu. And it's free! How crazy is that? The employee benefits are top-notch, which is part of what attracted me to this job. Though it was more the 401k matching and health insurance plan than the free lunches for employees, but still. It's a super-cool perk. The entire staff has access to this cafeteria too. Front-of-house, back-of-house, it doesn't matter. The general manager and the housekeeper will all use the same cafeteria, which I think is amazing and equalizing and all that stuff. It's a huge space, more like a buffet really, which will be necessary to accommodate the number of employees who will be working here once we're at full staff.

"Which guy?" Payton asks before taking a huge bite from a slice of pizza. She's a tiny slip of a thing despite chowing food with the metabolism of a boy in high school.

"The guy from the bar. From the other night."

"Shut up." She drops the pizza onto her plate and grins a grin that would make the Cheshire cat proud. "Here?" she questions, one brow arched in delight at the potential entertainment this will provide her.

"Of course here. I haven't been anywhere else today but here." I cut the chicken breast on my salad into smaller pieces before piercing one with my fork, ensuring I get a perfect portion of lettuce and dressing included.

"So he works here? Did you talk to him?"

"I think so, and no. I spotted him as I was walking through the hotel lobby with my orientation group. It's kind of cool being in here before it opens, isn't it?" It really is super-cool. Have you ever been in a Vegas casino after hours? No. No, you haven't, because once they open, they're open. Twenty-four hours a day, three hundred and sixty-five days a year. How many people get the opportunity to see a place like this before it opens? Not many, I'd bet.

The lobby was a bustle of activity. Construction workers on scaffolding making adjustments to the lighting while another group was tiling a decorative fountain the size of a small pool. Deliveries were being dropped at the lobby retail shops as empty cardboard boxes were being broken down and carted away.

The casino floor was much the same. Gaming tables in place, but vacant. Rows of slot machines were lit up but silent, and the entire floor was empty of people save for a bar in the center that was still under construction.

It smelled of new paint and carpet, but something else too. It smelled like a first day. Like potential and untapped energy and the whispered promise of an impending adventure.

It was eerily cool.

"Lydia, focus." Payton shakes the ice in her cup before taking a sip. "I need details!"

"I saw him in the lobby. I think he works here?" I say, but it's more of a question than a statement because I don't have a clue. "He was standing near the front doors with a couple of other guys. They were looking at a tablet and pointing at different spots in the lobby ceiling. Oh! Maybe he's in security or something? Shoot, I don't really know, but he looked like he belonged here. I suppose it's possible he's a contractor and I'll never cross paths with him again." I wrinkle my nose and shrug. It'll really suck if that was my one shot and I blew it. Even if he does work here, will I ever cross paths with him? This place is the equivalent of a small city. With thousands of employees, there will be plenty of people I rarely, if ever, see.

FOUR

LYDIA

I DON'T SEE HIM again that day, or the next. But I practice. By practice, I mean I have imaginary conversations with him so I'll be ready for a real conversation when I see him again. *Hey, remember me?* I say to myself in the mirror while drying my hair in the morning. *Oh, you! You work here? I work here!* I repeat this on my drive to work over and over until it sounds natural. If I'm at a stoplight I add a shoulder shrug and a hand gesture to the mix. *Hey, guy, would you believe I didn't catch your name?*

That last one needs work, admittedly. It sorta sucks that I have to call him Hey during these fantasy practice runs, but it is what it is. I thought about making up a name for him until I find out what his name is, but I didn't want to get attached to the wrong name. Like what if I call him Sam as a temporary placeholder, but it sticks somewhere in my brain and then during sex I accidentally call him Sam? Can you even imagine?

I can imagine it. I did imagine it, actually, and I cringed a thousand cringes. I imagined it was going well—the sex—and I was enjoying myself and he was enjoying himself and I was doing a really good job at the sexing and then, bam. I called out the wrong name and ruined everything. If you want the details, he was on top of me, mid-thrust, my ankle hooked around his back as I groaned, "Harder, Sam." Then he stopped, as one does when called the wrong name during sex. And I turned a hundred shades of red in total humiliation while he got dressed and left.

And I didn't even come.

So Hey will have to do until I find out his name. I figure if I accidentally call him Hey during sex I can at least salvage the situation before I offend him. So I bide my time, keep my eyes open and work on my imaginary conversations.

I'm confident it will pay off, because in my experience when you work hard and have a positive attitude, it pays off. If nothing else, practice makes perfect, so I'll be ready when I see him again.

ON FRIDAY I GET my own desk. I've never had a space of my own at work before, besides a locker in which to shove my handbag. It's actually a cubicle. I've got an entire five-by-five-foot space to call my own, complete with a name plate attached to the exterior of my cubicle wall.

Lydia Clark. I run my fingertip over the letters and grin before surveying my new space. I've got an L-shaped desk with a flat screen monitor already in place on the surface. There are three lined pads of paper, a package of pens and a six-pack of Post-It notes still wrapped in cellophane laying next to the keyboard. The cube walls are covered in some kind of taupe industrial-grade fabric, but they double as bulletin boards so I'll be able to pin notes for easy viewing.

Gah! I cannot wait to buy a cute pencil cup this weekend. Maybe I'll get a letter tray too, and colored file folders. I drop my handbag into the file cabinet drawer under the desk and text Payton.

LYDIA: Office supply shopping this weekend?!

PAYTON: Can't wait!

Oh, wow. I didn't think she'd care. She had almost no opinion about any of the stuff we got for our apartment. I wonder if I can get her to go to Ikea with me again.

LYDIA: Really??? Want to go to Ikea after work??

PAYTON: No, not really, nerd. It's our second weekend in Vegas. We are not spending Friday night at Ikea.

Oh. Well, maybe Saturday then.

I've got a team meeting in five minutes so I pocket my phone and make my way to the conference room. The second through fourth floors of this hotel are all office space. These floors aren't accessible from the guest elevators, so we're sorta hidden, like having a building within a building. We've got separate elevators from the employee entrance that service nothing but these three floors and the executive suites on thirty-four. Not that I've seen them—they're for senior-level employees who live on site. Can you even imagine?

My department—human resources—is on the

fourth floor along with legal, accounting, security and the executive offices. I'm a human resource associate, reporting to the director of human resources, who reports to the vice-president of human resources. If it sounds like a lot of people, it's because it is. I'm one of seven associates. We all started together this week and we will eventually be divided up and assigned as the lead contact by department. Housekeeping, food services, front desk and bell services, entertainment, recreation, retail and gaming. That's just the front-of-house stuff.

This place really is a world all of its own.

There's a break room on each floor with free coffee, so I stop there on my way to the conference room. It's got one of those fancy coffee machines that make lattes and espresso and hot cocoa and even regular coffee. God, working here is like a day at Disney for me! There's fruit and snacks and bottled water too, and—oh, my God. I stop dead. That guy. The break room has that guy too. I mean, he's here, in the break room. Not that he's stocked in the break room, like a free packet of peanuts, which are indeed stocked in the break room. *Gah, Lydia! Focus!*

I've taken two steps into the room, my heeled feet clicking on the linoleum and announcing my presence before I can do so myself. He's in the midst of uncapping a bottle of water and I have half a second to observe him before he notices me.

Half a second to confirm he just does it for me.

Why is that? All I've done is kiss him. Why does he have this effect on me? It's not like I'm so innocent that a kiss sends me reeling. I've kissed guys before and none of them made me feel like this. They made me feel, if I'm being honest, apathetic.

Hence why I'm still a virgin. Because why bother? If a guy makes you feel like you could take it or leave it, just why bother?

Yet this guy makes me feel like I could be actively promiscuous. Yup. When I see him I'm pretty sure I've got untapped slut potential. Holy all of everything that is good, why is he so attractive? It almost hurts to look directly at him. I feel all warm and turned on and weird.

He notices me and I see the flash of recognition or surprise in his eyes. I suppose it's a mixture of both, but it means he remembers me, doesn't it? It so does.

He says nothing, but his eyes remain on mine as he turns to face me. He brings the bottle to his lips and sips, seemingly unhurried, just watching me. His expression gives away nothing, and if I hadn't caught that brief look in his eye when he first saw me I'd think he didn't remember me, but he does. I know he does.

We're alone. Just us, an empty break room, the hum of the refrigerator and the smell of coffee permeating the air.

This is my chance.

"Oh, hey, um, so you work here?"

That's what I come up with for my big moment.

"We met the other day. Last weekend. Whatever." I add a stiff wave to the pile of awkward that just left my mouth.

"That we did," he replies with a small nod of his head. He recaps the water without looking at the bottle because his eyes never leave me. Gah, his freaking eyes. They do things to me. Dirty things, at least in my mind. His gaze dances across my face and I feel flush everywhere. I take a tentative couple of steps forward, my heels clicking against the floor. He has smart eyes. Intelligent. Insightful. He looks like a man capable of quick decisions. He looks like a man who doesn't miss the details.

"So you work here? I work here." I sound a little breathless when I say it. I exhale and try to pull myself together.

"Yes. It appears that we both work here."

I think I'm repeating myself. I need to move this along while I have the chance, before someone walks in or he takes off.

"So that was nice," I offer. "When we met."

"Nice?" I think his lip twists into the tiniest hint of a smirk when he speaks, one eyebrow quirked in question or amusement. I wish I could run my fingertip over that eyebrow. Examine the tiny line running across his forehead and whisper my fingers across his jaw.

"The kissing thing," I clarify. "In case you ever wanted to do it again."

His eyes widen and both brows rise, the smirk gone. Then he shakes his head a fraction and smiles. I'm amusing him. Shit. I must sound like a teenager, he's surely used to offers way beyond kissing.

"And whatever else you want," I amend quickly. "I mean, if you're interested."

"Jesus Christ." He says this slowly and not necessarily in a reverent way. The hand not holding the bottle of water comes up and drags across his jaw and then he tilts his head a little as if he's easing some kind of stress in his neck. The smirk is gone.

Wait. Have I got this all kinds of wrong? He did kiss me. Not that kissing me was some great declaration of interest, but he must have found me attractive enough to kiss. Surely suggesting we do it again shouldn't be so horrifying to him?

He drops the hand from his mouth. The water bottle in his other hand dangles from his fingertips, where he bounces it against his thigh. I wouldn't classify his actions as nervous. Not in the least. Restless, maybe. His expression is a little tortured if I had to pinpoint it. His eyes though... his eyes look interested. I might not be the most experienced girl in the world, but I think he looks at me with interest.

"Rhys!" a voice calls out from behind me and my eyes widen. I forgot to ask his name. Again. But it's Rhys. Rhys, Rhys, Rhys. I chant the name in my head and I like it. I like it a lot. A small smile tugs at my lips before I realize that I almost missed my chance to get his name for the second time. Smooth. Real smooth. I am such a freaking amateur.

I turn my head towards the voice to find the source is a tall good-looking man striding into the break room. Not as good-looking as Rhys, at least not to me, but I can see the appeal. He slaps Rhys on the back as he opens the fridge and grabs himself a bottle of water. He's dressed nicely—I realize now that they both are. Suits. Expensive suits. I'm familiar enough with fabric to spot the quality in those suits without touching them. They're put-together, the both of them. Well-knotted ties, polished shoes, chunky watches. They're hot. Walking, talking sex appeal.

Wait. What the hell did I just say to Rhys? *Whatever else you want?* Oh, my God. No. I feel my face start to heat up and I quickly drop my gaze to the linoleum floor and turn towards the fancy coffee maker. I grab a mug from the open shelving and set it in place on the machine, my hand shaking as I jab at the buttons. I did not practice that. My practice runs for when I saw him again did not include me offering to 'whatever else you want.' I didn't practice for interruptions either. Why didn't I have contingency plans for embarrassing myself and being interrupted? What am I supposed to do now?

I bite my lip and turn my head enough to see over my shoulder. Rhys' eyes flicker from the man to me and back again. I turn back to the coffee machine and jab at the buttons until the machine hisses and liquid splutters into the cup below. Then I grip the countertop in front of me until my knuckles turn white.

Maybe it wasn't that bad? What I said?

It was bad. And he didn't react, did he? Not really. What does that mean? Maybe he has a girlfriend? But he kissed me! A week ago he kissed me!

Behind me I hear the other man tell Rhys they're going to be late and then footsteps moving toward the doorway. I keep my hands where they are and watch whatever the heck I've selected as it drips into the cup.

Then they're gone.

I overhear my new supervisor Bethany exchanging hellos with them as they cross paths in the hallway a moment before she sails into the break room in their wake. I move my mug from the fancy coffee maker to the countertop and grab a stir stick as Bethany places a fresh mug onto the machine and smiles at me.

"Ohh, what did you make?" she asks, nodding at my cup.

"A latte of some kind," I say and force a smile before taking a sip. I want to pour it down the sink because I'm in no condition to carry a mug full of hot liquid and no longer need the caffeine boost, but it would be weird to pour it out with her standing here watching me. I tear open a packet of sweetener and add it to my mug before speaking again. "Hey, do you know that guy who was just here? Rhys?" I manage to ask it so casually I might deserve a badge in being breezy. "Do you know where he works?"

"Rhys?" Bethany turns to me with a look of confusion on her face.

"I know he works here," I clarify. "What does he do?" I recall that my department shares this floor with legal and security. And accounting. But he looked more like a lawyer than an accountant.

I'm an idiot. As if anyone looks like an accountant or a lawyer.

"He's the general manager," Bethany replies and I pause, stir stick dangling from my fingertips over the trash can.

This is bad. Deep down I'm pretty sure there is only one general manager in the management structure, but I try all the same. "Of which department?" I manage to keep my voice steady, my eyes on the stir stick. It's landed atop a banana peel inside the trash can. There's a soda can beside it and I'm annoyed at whomever didn't drop it into the recycling bin. It only takes a second.

"Of the property," Bethany says and I lose about a decade from my lifespan in that moment.

FIVE

I MADE IT THROUGH the rest of the day, though I have no idea how I did not perish on the spot, except to say that death by mortification must not be a quick way to go.

I stood in the break room with my new boss while she clarified that Rhys is the general manager—of the entire resort.

That was bad.

It got worse.

The resort is owned by Sutton Travel Corporation, which I knew—of course I knew that. I was thrilled to get a job at a large company with excellent benefits and I did my research. Sutton is headquartered out of Britain and operates in over fifty countries. Hotels, tour groups, cruise lines and now a luxury resort on the Las Vegas Strip. They've been in business for decades. They're known for nurturing talent and promoting from within.

The company was founded by William Sutton.

Rhys's grandfather.

So.

So that makes him some kind of part-owner, doesn't it?

I'm getting fired. Totally getting fired. I'm in human resources and I propositioned my boss' boss' boss for sex. What is wrong with me? Seriously. I'm better than this. I'm not that kind of girl. I'm good! I dot the i's and I cross the t's! I pay my bills early. I recycle! I do not proposition my boss for sex. Ugh. I'm so gross.

I squeeze my eyes shut every time I remember the train wreck that was me attempting to flirt. My first week at my first job and I'm going to get fired. I spent the afternoon wondering if I should fire myself. Should I just go ahead and process the paperwork? We covered the company process for severing employment in training yesterday so I know how to do it.

I didn't know what to do. So instead I carried my mug of whatever latte down the hall to conference room 4C. I kept my eyes down as I sat through a meeting with my team about the training set to begin on Monday. With the resort opening soon, the front-of-house staff are scheduled to begin in waves over the next three weeks. Meaning endless paperwork. Endless W-4's and I-9's that need to be completed. Checklists a mile long multiplied by several thousand new hires who will all need to start at virtually the same time. Early enough to ensure they're trained to company standards, but not so early that we've employees on payroll before the doors open. Easy. I took notes on everything, my mind whirling with a legion of thoughts, not all of which were on state regulations and benefit meetings.

Then I slunk back to my desk, waiting for the ax to fall. I jumped every time anyone walked past my cube, expecting it to be Bethany with a sad smile on her face as she asked if she could have a word with me.

It didn't happen. I even stayed an extra half hour to give her every opportunity to fire me before the weekend. You know, in case she was running behind schedule? But eventually I noticed her office light was off, so I assumed she'd left and if I was getting fired it wasn't happening until Monday. I grabbed my handbag and left my dirty mug on my desk for the entire weekend because the thought of going back to the break room gave me post-traumatic stress. It caused me some stress to leave a dirty mug sitting on my desk too, but you gotta pick your battles.

Once I was safely locked in my car I texted Payton and told her I had errands to run and I'd be home in a few hours. I needed time in my happy place before I'd be ready to talk about this day.

Then I pulled up the Goodwill store finder for Greater Las Vegas from my phone. I realize it's not the usual happy place for a twenty-two-year-old, but I'm not the most usual of twenty-two-year-olds.

It only takes me a moment to realize I've moved to the holy land of Goodwill stores. There are so many of them! There were only a few near my parents' house back in Knoxville, but there's at least a dozen here! And what is this, a Goodwill outlet center? No way! Wait. Dang it. The outlet center is only open on weekdays during work hours. Well, at least I have something to look forward to when I get fired. I'll be able to shop at the Goodwill outlet center as much as I want.

There are two locations between work and my apartment. I plug in the address of the first and pull out of the parking garage onto Las Vegas Boulevard.

My limited experience in this city is that traffic is always bad on the Strip, but luckily I've got less than a quarter-mile before I can cut over to Convention Center Drive and get out of this mess. Fifteen minutes later I'm pulling into a strip mall off of Maryland Parkway. I find a space near the door and survey the store from outside. It looks like a good one—sometimes you can just tell these things, you know?

I sigh as I turn off my car and lock it. It's so pretty here. I know most people don't think that about Vegas, but it is. Once you get off the Strip it's lovely, all palm trees and desert landscapes. I hope I get to stay. I haven't blown it. I hope I don't have to call my dads and tell them I'm moving back home.

I step through the automatic doors and breathe in the reassuring smell of mothballs and dust as I grab a cart. Of course I'll need a cart. I make note that the color of the week is blue, which means anything with a blue tag I get for fifty percent off. I tap my fingers on the cart handle as I survey the store before making my way to the first rack of adult clothing. The sizing doesn't really matter because I'm going to launder everything and tear it apart. I don't even particularly care if it's women's clothing. I've turned men's suits into all sorts of things. Scarves, handbags, a cape. Once I made a dress out of a suit jacket.

Sometimes I find a great piece, but mostly it's junk I have to wade through and rework. I enjoy it. I find it very satisfying to take something that's been discarded and rework it into something new.

My old Girl Trooper leader, Mrs. Barnes, taught me how to sew. It's not a skill most young women learn anymore. It hasn't been for some time, I suppose. I could use new fabric, but fabric is crazy expensive. Plus it's so much more fun to hunt for it, like a treasure. I exhale and start at the end of a row, quickly flipping through the hangers. The tiny screech they make as they slide against the metal bar calms me. Slide, slide, slide. Pause. Examine. Repeat. Three rows in, I'm in the zone. The stress of the day eases while I focus on nothing but checking labels and prices, eyeballing if an item will have enough usable fabric to do anything with.

I'm halfway through the women's clothing when I look up and spot the hanging rack of sheets. Old patterned sheets, folded and hanging from pants hangers. I abandon the clothing racks as an idea forms. Pajamas. I could cut up the flat sheets and make pajama bottoms. I could use the wide cuffs from the pillowcases and the top sheet on the hemline of the pants. I could make shorts with the smaller leftover. Heck, I bet I could get at least one pair of shorts, a pair of pants and even a spaghetti-strap tank top out of each sheet! I've got a pattern at home, and elastic and everything else I need. I can spend the entire weekend measuring and pinning and cutting and sewing.

Not thinking about the reaction I had to him. A reaction I've never felt before, not like that. Not thinking about the fact that he's my boss' boss' boss. Not thinking about the way he just stared at me this afternoon when I practically threw myself at him.

Which will be impossible. I'm positive the words 'and whatever else you want' will still be replaying themselves in my mind when I'm eighty years old.

Payton texts while I'm checking out. She doesn't know about my Goodwill hobby, so I avoid her question about where I'm at and tell her I'm on my way home. I've managed to spend over two hours in this store so I won't have time to stop at another one before closing anyway. She tells me to meet her at the pool when I get home. Says the hot tub is filled with hot men.

I tell her I have laundry to do, which is not a lie. I've got sheets to wash before I can start cutting them up.

"YOU'RE NOT GETTING fired, relax."

This tidbit of wisdom comes from Payton. I've been home for a couple of hours, washing and drying sheets. Payton returned from the pool to find me ironing them and just about lost her shit. She attempted to institute a roommate rule banning the ironing of sheets on a Friday night. Or on any day that ends in -day. I explained that I needed to iron the sheets as the story of my terrible, awful, very bad day tumbled out of me.

"I'm so getting fired. I work in human resources and I propositioned the general manager." My cheeks still get hot when I say it out loud. Or think about it.

"You likely made his day." Payton has showered and changed into yoga pants and a tank. Her blonde hair is still wet as she sits on a barstool at our kitchen island and watches me work. I've taken over our dining table with my cutting mat and sewing supplies, neatly lined up beside me as I work. I don't look up as I slide the rotary cutter across a layer of fabric, making a perfect cut on what is soon to become a pair of pajama shorts.

"Made his day? I don't think sexually harassing him made his day." I remove the pattern from the material and stick the pins into my pincushion, ensuring none of them go rogue and end up on the floor.

"Simmer down. You did not sexually harass him. Also, I still don't understand what is happening here," she says, waving a hand at the table. "You're turning old sheets into pajamas?"

"Yes. You want a pair?"

"Err, not really." Her eyebrows come together and her expression is all doubt.

"You will when I'm done," I assure her.

"If you say so. Now let's get back to Rhys."

"There's nothing to get back to. I've told you everything and I'm getting fired on Monday. I should be packing, not making pajamas."

"First of all, you're not getting fired. Second of all, you're not moving even if you get fired."

"You just said I wasn't getting fired!" I screech.

"You're not. But I know you like to think about the worst-case scenario, so let's do that."

That's true. I do enjoy thinking about all possible options. "Okay," I agree, sinking into a kitchen chair. I fiddle with the pincushion to keep my hands busy and wait for Payton to start.

"Okay, so let's say you walk in on Monday and you get fired." She gets up as she talks and walks to our pantry, returning with a box of Cheez-Its.

"Yeah." I nod. I've already visualized at least four different ways it could happen.

"So you'll walk back to your car, drive home and cry. I'll pick up pizza after work and we'll cry some more. Then on Tuesday you'll get a new job." She pops a Cheez-It into her mouth and shrugs one shoulder as if this solves everything.

"Payton." I groan and roll my eyes. "It doesn't work like that."

"It works exactly like that. We're in Las Vegas. There are jobs everywhere," she says, flipping open the lid of her laptop. "There are three hundred and thirty-four job listings on this job site using the keyword 'human resources.' Let's assume that two hundred of them are relevant, and assume you're qualified for fifty of them. That's fifty jobs you could apply for tonight!"

Well. I shrug. "It doesn't mean I'd get any of them."

"No, it doesn't," Payton agrees, snapping her laptop shut. "But you could waitress. You're a hot twenty-two-year-old with a great body, you'd kill it in tips. You'd probably make double what they're paying you at the Windsor."

"You think so?"

"I just talked to some girl at the pool. She said she quit her job teaching because she makes twice as much as a cocktail waitress at the Wynn."

"Shut up."

"It's true."

"Are you sure she wasn't a hooker?"

"She wasn't a hooker. But that's always a backup option for you." Payton says this with complete sincerity and it makes me burst into giggles. "Are you okay now? I can't go to bed until I know you're not going to stay up all night making sheet pajamas."

"I'm still mortified, Payton." I groan and drop my head into my hands, my hair falling in a curtain around my spread fingers. "I just stood there babbling about how good the kissing thing was and then I offered—I don't even know what I offered. I think I offered him carte blanche, because what does the word 'whatever' even include? It sort of implies anything and everything, doesn't it? I might have offered spanking and anal for all I know."

"Oh, you definitely offered spanking and anal."

"Argggh," I groan from behind my hands.

"You made his day, young grasshopper. Trust me on this. Besides, I saw the guy, you cannot be the only woman who's ever propositioned him. He's hot as fuck."

"So perhaps he's so used to women coming onto him that he won't even remember today?"

"Totally." She nods seriously and pops another Cheez-It.

"Doubtful, but I appreciate you lying to me in order to talk me off the ledge."

SIX

WHATEVER ELSE YOU want.

I drum my fingertips on the conference table and try to focus on the meeting Canon is leading about security, but I can't. I can't because my mind is on Lydia.

This pisses me off because I'm not the type of man to be distracted by pussy.

Especially not good-girl pussy.

Goddammit.

This girl makes me feel something. Irritation mostly, because I'm thinking about her instead of this meeting.

Whatever else you want. If you're interested.

I must groan out loud replaying those words in my head because Canon shoots me a look before refocusing his attention on the president of the company we purchased our surveillance equipment from. They're discussing a technology package that uncovers connections between people—connections that could be used to fraudulently game the house. The moment you appear on one of our cameras the image will be fed into the data mine and begin making connections, meaning when a customer

41

takes a seat at a table the system will immediately attempt to draw a connection between the customer and the dealer. It also checks all known databases for mug shots, missing persons, and registered firearm holders. Social media sites, of course. Yearbooks, any photo uploaded to a public database. If the security system can't identify who you are within fourteen seconds an alert is sent to the security team because it means there is no recorded image of you anywhere on the Internet. And that's questionable as fuck.

Lawson interjects with a string of legal questions, questions I should be thinking about as well, but I'm not. Good thing Lawson is adept at his job.

My attention is shot to hell. It's on a sweet twenty-something who makes my dick hard. Harder than it should be based on the limited interactions we've had. Way harder than it should be for a girl like her. Yet my mind drifts to the memory of how her lips felt on mine, so soft, so eager. The way she smelled of sunshine and tasted of peppermint lip balm. The way her eyelashes fluttered against her cheeks before she turned her big green eyes on me, looking at me like I hung the moon. Her pupils softened with arousal as she blinked when I broke off the kiss, holding her steady so she didn't topple over. So I wouldn't be tempted to press my hard-on into her stomach.

A hard-on from a simple goddamned kiss.

I don't do good girls. Not anymore. Not ever, really.

What I do is temporary. Beautiful, fast, temporary women. Which has made Vegas a perfect fit for me. It's a never-ending refill of women looking for their 'what happens in Vegas stays in Vegas' moments. Then they leave and return to their tranquil lives, or their high-powered jobs, or their boyfriends. I don't know, and I don't care.

When not tourists, strippers. I like hookers too. That's crass, I know. I'm a piece of shit, I know. I can do better, I know.

I know, I know, I know.

I'm not unhappy with my life. I'm not searching for anything, or anyone. I'm not. I've simply learned there are some women you can ask certain things of and some you can't. 'Spread your legs. Bend over. Choke on it. Get out.' Those kind of things.

Fuck. Lydia was using the break room closest to my office, so she must work on four. Just fucking great.

Whatever else you want.

We don't want the same things, Lydia.

SEVEN

LYDIA

"WHAT TIME DO YOU want to go to Ikea?" Payton yawns as she passes me on her way into the kitchen.

"You want to go to Ikea with me?" I look up in surprise as I raise the presser foot on my sewing machine and pull the fabric free. I snip the threads and stand, holding the completed pajama bottoms in front of me for inspection.

"Of course I don't want to go, I'm just that good of a friend," Payton quips as she pours herself a cup of coffee. She turns, mug in hand, and watches me examine the PJs. "Hey, those are really cute." She sets her coffee down and takes the bottoms from me, holding them up against her hips.

"Ha! I told you you'd want a pair when they were done!"

"So you're a secret sewing ninja or something?" She pulls the pants away from her hips and examines the wide hem I made from the border of a set of pillowcases. "I'm starting to think you were picking up life skills while I was making out with boys in the backs of cars."

"I think I'll make a dress next."

"Okay, let's not get crazy." Payton folds the

pajama bottoms in half then drapes them over a kitchen chair. "Wait, how many pairs have you made so far? You did sleep last night, right?" She frowns as she picks up a pair of pajama shorts with a satin drawstring bow.

"I've only been up for a couple hours. These are just easy to make. Look, I made a matching top for that one." I hold up a simple tank with spaghetti straps and a scrap of eyelet lace added to the scoop neckline.

Payton takes the tank from me and examines it, the straps dangling from her fingertips. "Huh. What else do you know how to do? Do you churn butter? Can you knit us an afghan? Oh, my God, I bet you know how to bake a Thanksgiving turkey, don't you?" She drops into a seat at the table and places a hand on my forearm. "Lydia, did you earn the 1950's housewife badge?" She blinks, eyes wide with inquiry.

"Pfft, there is no such thing as a 1950's housewife badge, which you would know if you hadn't gotten kicked out. I did earn the dinner party badge though."

"Oh, holy shit." She drops her hand and leans back, looking at me in something akin to horror. "I was joking. There's a dinner party badge? Stop."

"There is. Also, knitting has become trendy again, just so you know. And no, I don't know how to knit. Maybe we can take a class together?" I'm teasing because I don't think there's a chance Payton is signing up for a knitting class with me.

"I don't really think that would be my cup of Coke," she replies.

"Cup of Coke? Do you mean not your cup of tea?"

"No. I don't like tea." She yawns and examines

another pair of pajama shorts.

"It's just a saying, Payton. You don't need to replace tea with something you like."

"Hmm. I don't think that's right. Anyway, Ikea?"

"Do I really deserve new desk accessories if I'm getting fired?"

"Ugh, enough with the getting fired." Payton groans into her coffee cup. "It's not happening. And spending the weekend making sheet pajamas is not happening either. Let's go to the pool, then we'll go to Ikea and grab dinner."

———

PAYTON IS SLY. WHICH is why I didn't realize that 'go to Ikea and grab dinner' was really just trickery for dragging me out to socialize. Oh, we went to Ikea. She even drove. Then she drove us to the bar.

"Really, Payton?" I ask when she pulls into a parking spot at Hennigan's. "You said we were going to dinner."

"What? We can order chicken fingers here. That counts as dinner." She flips the visor down as she digs a lip gloss from her handbag and uncaps it. "A couple guys from the pool are going to meet up with us."

"This is a date? You set me up on a date?" I turn to her in confusion while trying to figure out how she managed to make plans for tonight while I was with her at the pool. She's clearly much better at this sort of thing than I am. I wonder which guys? No one I saw today compared to Rhys, but perhaps it's time I stopped being so picky. Maybe my problem is that I'm unreasonable?

"Uh, no. It's not a date." She shakes her head, raising a skeptical eyebrow in my direction. "It's a couple of guys who live at our apartment complex meeting us at this bar, which is less than a mile from where we all live."

"Oh, okay."

"Relax, grasshopper. It's just drinks."

"Great idea."

"Really?" Now she's openly dubious, doing nothing to hide her narrowed eyes or pursed lips.

"Really." I flip my own visor down and examine my reflection. "Well played, just warn me next time so I can wear something besides a t-shirt that says 'Let's Taco 'Bout It.'" I remove the hair band from my hair and shake my hair out, combing my fingers through it. I got some sun today and I put on mascara before we left, so good enough. "But tomorrow I'm making sheet pajamas all day," I tell her, waving my hands in the air, complete with wiggly fingers, "and I don't want to hear a word about it."

"Fine. But this was disappointingly easy. I was kinda gearing up to drag you inside," Payton says as we exit the car. The warmth hits the moment I slide a leg out of the car. It's about seventy degrees at eight PM, but yes, it's a dry heat, as they say.

"Sorry to disappoint," I tell her as I slam the passenger door shut. "If it helps, I'm not making out with anyone this time though. And that is not a challenge. It's not happening."

"Why not? The best way to get over someone is to get under someone else."

"I was never under Rhys."

"I think it's figurative."

Once inside, we grab a table and order a couple of

beers. I don't particularly love beer, but what the heck, when in Rome. I wonder if they drink beer in Rome? Maybe that's not a great analogy. Maybe I should have ordered wine? I wasn't sure if chicken fingers went with wine. Well, never mind—my beer has arrived.

Josh and Dan have arrived too. I recognize them from the pool, Payton reminding me who is who before they reach our table. A third guy arrives a few minutes after them, one I don't recognize but who seems to be a friend of theirs. I don't catch his name, and he doesn't appear to have much interest in getting mine, so I don't bother. In any case, Payton wasn't lying. This isn't a setup or a date. It's just some people getting together to have a drink, maybe become friends. Maybe more, who knows?

Socializing is hard.

I don't have any particular phobias about socializing, nothing like that. I'm quite good at social etiquette and making friends. I earned every life skill badge one can obtain during my Girl Trooper days.

But bars are different. Distributing coasters to avoid drink rings on the tabletop is not considered a social asset, for example.

Which is ridiculous, but whatever. I dip a chicken finger into a plastic ramekin of honey mustard and listen to what Josh is telling me about his job. He seems interested in me. Not aggressively interested, just normally interested, which is nice.

He's attractive.

He's attentive.

He's available.

I feel nothing.

But maybe I will feel something, if I try harder. Maybe that's how this works. Maybe it's not always instant, blinding, inexplicable lust.

Like it was with Rhys. Why was it so instant with Rhys? So annoyingly instant. The first time I saw him I was in lust with him before he'd even caught me looking at him.

Focus on Josh.

I order another drink and focus. On Josh. Nice Josh. Age-appropriate Josh. Not my boss' boss' boss Josh.

I looked Rhys up last night. Of course I did. Once Payton pried the cutting ruler out of my hand and sent me to bed, I lay in the dark doing internet searches on Rhys Dalton. I'm not sure what I was looking for exactly, it's not as if I was going to find an article about some other girl who embarrassed herself in front of him worse than I did.

Okay, yes, I did look for that article. It doesn't exist, obviously. Then I Googled 'embarrassing myself in front of my crush' just to cheer myself up. Two stories in I decided it was best I stop reading in case I was subconsciously storing additional ways to embarrass myself.

Anyway, I didn't find much on Rhys. A few boring business things. I couldn't find a wife or girlfriend, but it's not like he had a Facebook page for me to troll through. The only social account I could find for him was on LinkedIn and that site was really not designed for creeping on your boss. Not in a meaningful way, at least.

He's thirty-four. A little old for me, possibly. But it's not as if I have daddy issues, so I think it's okay. I had two dads growing up. Two perfect dads who adored me and each other. My childhood was the opposite of dysfunctional. It was totally functional, in a nonconventional way. So no, I don't have any need to be daddied and if I want to lose my virginity to a man who's possibly a little too old for me, that's really my decision, isn't it?

"Lydia?" Josh is asking me something and I'm not paying the best of attention. Because I'm thinking about freaking Rhys.

"Yes?" I smile at Josh and renew my effort to pay attention to him. He has nice hair. And he's nice. And he's speaking to me and would probably respond if I offered him whatever he wanted instead of just staring at me as if I had not just made a very generous offer.

"Darts?" He nods to a dart board near our table. He has kind eyes and he seems genuinely interested in my response, in me saying yes.

"Sure." I place my beer on a coaster and tap the tabletop with my hand. "Let's do it."

By it, I mean darts not sex. For now. But maybe I'll change my mind. Not like tonight, let's not get crazy. But maybe Josh will grow on me. Maybe we'll become friends. He's sort of funny and I do like him. Maybe the magical and elusive lust cupid will strike, you never know.

EIGHT

RHYS

"WHY IN THE FUCK ARE we at a bar in Henderson?" Canon physically grimaces and shakes his head in confusion as I slide my car into a parking spot in front of Hennigan's.

"My buddy owns the place. I told him I'll stop in to check it out."

"Yeah. Yeah, you did. Which is why you brought your cousin here last weekend."

Fuck. I forgot he knew about that.

"It's just a quick drink, Canon," I say, deflecting. "We'll go to Strippers Strippers Strippers as soon as we're done."

"Don't be an asshole. You know it's called Double Diamonds, not Strippers Strippers Strippers. And you also know it's my favorite of the strip clubs. Have some respect for my hobbies."

I stop, meeting Canon at the bumper of my car as I hit the remote lock for the car. He's not wrong. I have no idea what the fuck we're doing at a bar in Henderson either. Not really. Am I hoping I might see her again? I know I'll see her again. On Monday, at work. Where I will keep my kisses and my filthy thoughts to myself because she's twenty-fucking-

53

two. And my employee.

Yeah.

Twenty-two.

I'm a pervert for even thinking about her. An asshole for using her employment file to find the information in the first place. It's just... why did she have to offer that? *Whatever else you want.* I want. Of course I want. I'm not a saint for fuck's sake.

I'd be a liar in addition to a deviant if I didn't admit that the relative inexperience that comes with her age is a huge turn-on. So fucking confident in my ability to be better than anything she'd have experienced thus far.

"Canon, what is that rule about age limits?"

"What rule?"

I pocket the key fob and run a hand over the back of my neck in agitation. "The thing about how young you can go? It's half your age plus five, right? God, why am I asking you?" I twist my neck and stare at the entrance to Hennigan's.

The look he gives me makes me sorry I brought it up. I should have asked my cousin—that pretentious British bastard would've had the answer.

"It's half plus seven, not five. And it's for dating, not fucking. There are no rules for fucking, except that she's eighteen. Though eighteen is really, really questionable and if you're fucking a teenager I need you to stop and evaluate your life."

"Right. Half plus seven." I nod like it doesn't matter, already regretting bringing this up with Canon.

"Tell me we're talking about a twenty-one-year-old. Tell me you don't have your balls ready to blow over a teenager."

"Jesus, relax. I don't. Never mind, we're not

talking about this." I nod my head towards the pub door and start walking.

"This is why Double Diamonds is my club of choice. Vince doesn't hire unless they're twenty-one."

"What?"

"Great benefits too."

"What?" I stop so I can look at Canon. "What the fuck are you talking about?"

"The strippers at Double Diamonds. Comprehensive benefits package. Health insurance, tuition reimbursement. No stage fees. Did you know most clubs charge the dancers just to work?" He spits this last part out, his tone indicating his disgust at the patriarchy of the modern strip club worker.

"How..." I hesitate, as I stare at him, speechless. "Why do you know this?"

"I golfed with Vince last week."

"Great. Glad to hear you're making new friends."

"Don't be jealous. You were busy." Canon checks his watch and glances at Hennigan's. "God. I hope your teenager isn't hanging out in a bar."

"Will you shut the fuck up? She's not a teenager. And she's not mine."

Not mine, and not at the bar.

I notice it as soon as we're through the door, as if I expected her to be in the same seat she was in last weekend, waiting for me. Possibly because I know damn well that she lives down the street after my perusal of her employment file.

I'd only wanted to confirm which department she was in, a flicker of hope that she'd simply been on four for a meeting and seeing her would not be a common occurrence. But no. She's in human resources, assigned to cubicle 4W-28, putting her on the west side of the fourth floor. Way too close to my office for comfort.

Goddammit, I walked away for a reason. I didn't fuck her in Brady's office last weekend, even though I wanted to, because I'm not in the habit of making bad decisions. So I sent her home, where she belonged. Far away from a man like me, a man interested in one thing when the soft blinking of her eyes and the wide-eyed optimism on her face told me she was interested in something different. Then she shows up in my office. Nearly two hundred thousand people employed on the Vegas Strip and she's working in my casino. Sitting eighty feet from my office.

Fuck.

I don't need the distraction and she sure as hell doesn't need me. Opening this resort is my focus. Nothing else, no one else. This is my moment. This is my time to make a lasting contribution to the family company. This venture was my brainchild. I'm the one who brought it to the board. I'm the one who lined up the investment money. I'm the one who spent the last four years eating, living, breathing with the sole goal of making the Windsor the most profitable arm of the family business.

Me.

Besides, I fuck. I don't take women to dinner and escort them home to Connecticut to meet my parents.

Focused.

I'm a privileged son of a bitch. No, that's not right. I'm the privileged son of an heiress. My great-grandfather started a company that's ensured financial stability for generations. Each generation since, instead of resting, has grown the company larger. Bigger, better, more successful.

My mother has been running the North American division of Sutton Corporation for two decades. She's a force to be reckoned with and, in her fifties, not ready to step aside. My cousin took over as CEO of the company two years ago.

I could have fucked off for the rest of my life and it wouldn't matter. The company would have kept moving without me. I'm not an integral part, not like my mother, or my cousin, or my uncle running the cruise lines. My twenties were a struggle finding my place in this conglomeration. A place that would matter, a chapter header instead of a footnote.

The Windsor is my chapter header, my legacy.

It's not lost on me that my lasting contribution to humanity will be the self-indulgent opening of a luxury hotel on the Las Vegas Strip, not charity or healthcare reform or the abolition of racial disparity or funding public education.

Brady's behind the bar, more observing than bartending, so when he spots us arrive he comes over and we do the obligatory backslap handshake.

"Two weekends in a row. Wow." Brady folds his arms and leans against the bar top. "You're either really impressed with my microbrew or you're back for the girl."

Thanks, Brady.

"We sure as fuck did not come out to Henderson for beer," Canon mutters as he slides onto a stool. "You do card here, right?"

I'm about to tell Canon to fuck off when Brady tilts his head across the room. So she is here. I'm flooded with a rush of adrenaline, and something else, something different. There's a sense of exhilaration at seeing her again, a wasted emotion for a man just looking to fuck. As if I'm a teenager and this might be the first time I get my hand down a girl's pants, when I'm not and it's not.

Perhaps I just need to get her out of my system. Maybe just a taste, a quick fuck. A good time for both of us and then we move on. On Monday it's back to business. I turn in my seat, scanning the bar as Brady sets a couple of drafts in front of us. I locate her, pulling darts from a targeted cork board, her dark hair spilling down her back, the lighting picking up the highlights woven throughout her hair. She's in a denim skirt, the material snug over the curve of her ass, and the sight makes my eager fingers tighten around the glass in my hand. It doesn't help matters when she lifts up on her tiptoes to grab at a dart just out of her reach, her ass rising that much higher as she reaches.

She's tiny, and it makes me feel protective towards her in some antiquated bullshit way. As if she might need me to carry her over a puddle or buy her something pretty. She needs neither. She'd be easy to lift though, her legs spread around my hips as I sank into her, my hands gripping her ass as I bounced her up and down on my cock, her hands tugging my hair as she begged me for more, more, more.

In my mind she begs. Tiny whimpers. *Please, Rhys. More, Rhys.*

She turns, flashing a smile at someone behind her. Her smile is wide, a strand of hair falling across her cheek and her eyes sparkling with laughter. Her face is devoid of any visible makeup, which only serves to make her look younger and less calculated in any art of seduction.

As if her objectives are so much less intentional

than most women. Less rehearsed. Or maybe she simply has no clue how she affects men, but that can't be right.

My eyes land on what she's smiling at. Or whom. A man. Why the hell am I surprised? As if she's been waiting around since—yesterday—when she offered me whatever I wanted with her? Seriously, what the fuck?

I snort and turn back to my drink.

Then I turn back to Lydia.

Canon watches me and rolls his eyes. "Okay, wow."

"Fuck off." I bring the glass to my lips and sip, eyes on my good girl as she tosses a dart. She says something that makes that man laugh and I wonder if they came together. Where the hell is the pushy blonde she was with last week? I assumed, like the arrogant asshole I am, that she'd be here with her friend. Just waiting for me to arrive and repeat the 'kissing thing,' as she called it. I take another sip and scan the bar until I find the blonde. She's at a table with two guys. Which means there are five of them and it's not a date. Or it's one hell of a kinky date.

"Lydia Clark. Recent graduate of LSU. New hire at the Windsor. Twenty-two." Canon gives me a dramatic wink at that detail before continuing, "Had a dog named Scout growing up—"

I stop watching Lydia to interrupt Canon. "How do you know that?"

"You pay me for security, remember? I know everything." He gives me a knowing look, as if he's some kind of clairvoyant.

It's creepy.

"Also I just took a picture of her and ran it through the software we're using for the casino," he adds, which makes a hell of a lot more sense than him being omniscient.

"Yeah, but how do you know about her dog? That wasn't on her employment file."

"No, it's on an Instagram post from last week," he says, looking at his phone. "Hashtag TBT," he reads aloud. "It's a Throwback Thursday post with a picture of a ten-year-old Lydia and her dog. See?" He turns his phone in my direction and I snatch it out of his hand with more aggravation than is necessary, but he's goading me for his own amusement. There she is. Tweenaged Lydia with a dog. She's in a Girl Trooper uniform. Jesus Christ. I toss Canon's phone onto the bar top in disgust.

"You know, when you're forty she'll be twenty-eight."

"Yeah, I get it, I'm old. She's young." I wonder if they really are on a fivesome date? Maybe that's what the kids are into now.

"No, asshole. I'm saying that when you're forty half your age plus seven is twenty-seven. When you're forty Lydia will be twenty-eight."

"So if I can avoid touching her for six years I won't be a pervert? Thanks, that's helpful."

"I'm saying it all evens up in the next few years so why delay the gratification now?"

"I'm no morality expert, but I don't think that's right."

Across the bar the guy Lydia's playing darts with stands behind her and places one hand on her hip and another over the hand holding the dart. Her dart-throwing skills are fine so it's a lame-ass move on his part.

I wonder if she'll kiss him. I wonder if she'll offer him more.

I wonder why in the fuck I care.

I wonder if I'm having some kind of goddamn midlife crisis. It defies all reasonable logic. Why do I need to touch this particular girl? What does it matter? There are no fewer than ten women at Double Diamonds who would go home with me tonight—women who have gone home with me in the past. Women I pay money to so I can kick them out five minutes after I come.

Women who don't look at me as if they might expect better out of me.

Fuck.

"We should go," I murmur, but I'm still watching Lydia.

"Yup," Canon agrees, but he makes no move to get up. He doesn't even take his eyes off the game playing on one of the bar TV's.

She must feel me beside her before she sees me because she turns a moment before I take her hand in mine. Her eyes widen in surprise, her lashes fluttering against her cheeks as she quickly blinks. Her lips part, come together again as a smile breaks out. She flushes, the color high on her cheeks, and there's that look again. Expectation. God help me, she looks at me with hope.

What am I doing?

She has to tilt her head back to look at me because I'm standing on top of her, with her soft hand enveloped in my own larger, rougher one. I squeeze and her breathing increases, her eyes sparkling, a look of raw anticipation on her face.

"Rhys?" she asks, and hearing my name on her lips makes my pulse kick up and my cock harden.

I don't respond, instead giving her hand a tug and moving us towards Brady's office. The moment we clear the doorway I'm on her, a tangle of lips and tongue and a fistful of hair.

Until Brady's chair scrapes across the floor. Lydia breaks away from me with a squeak.

"Again with my office. I'll see myself out," Brady mutters as he passes us, the door clicking shut behind him.

I laugh and Lydia blushes.

"Who's the guy?"

"Who?" She blinks at me in utter confusion and I'm gratified that she can't remember a man she was talking to two minutes ago.

"Darts," I remind her and she looks down at her hand where she's still clutching the darts for her turn. She opens her palm and stares at them, then back to me.

"Josh?" she answers, but she says it like a question, like she's possibly already forgotten his name. Good girl. "Just a guy from my apartment complex. We met him at the pool today."

She's gotten some sun today, I note, a sprinkling of freckles covering her nose and cheeks, and I'm annoyed at the idea of stupid Josh seeing her wet and covered in a scrap of fabric.

"We have a pool at the hotel," I tell her.

"Yeah, and I have a pool at my apartment complex," she replies with a small laugh, as if we're simply comparing amenities, her eyes searching my face for some clue as to what I'm on about.

I don't know, so I kiss her instead. I take the darts from her and toss them in the direction of Brady's desk.

I kiss her again and she leans in closer, placing her hands on my chest. Her touch is light, shy? But her lips are eager. Her lips are pliant and soft and sweet. Her kisses feel like a preview to what sex would feel like with her. Hungry. Intimate. Exploratory.

I walk us backwards towards the couch, saying a silent prayer of thanks to Brady for having the foresight to have a couch in his office. She lands on my chest, her body soft and light on top of mine, but it's her eyes that interest me. They widen, as if she's surprised at where she's found herself, which she should not be after propositioning me just yesterday. But perhaps that's not normal behavior for her. Perhaps there's something about me specifically that makes her do things outside of her norm.

I find I like that idea.

The look of surprise lasts only a second, replaced with a slow smile that spreads across her entire face. If I thought she was pretty before, it's nothing compared to this moment. Her tongue peeks out to wet her lips and then she ducks her head, a tiny giggle escaping before she looks up again. She peeks at me from underneath her lashes and there's a spark of excitement in her eyes now, her hands sliding up my chest, her fingers splaying outwards in exploration, the tips massaging like a very happy kitten.

And then she flexes her hips.

God help me, she flexes her hips. A tiny rolling motion pushing her pelvis against my thigh, seeking friction, seeking more. I slide my hand over her hip to palm her ass and she does it again. Harder this time, more deliberate, yet I don't think she's aware she's doing it at all. Her hands are busy feeling my chest through the fabric of my shirt and her eyes are busy examining the places she follows with a kiss. My neck. My right eyebrow. My left earlobe. She pauses there, pulling my flesh between her teeth with a gentle tug before following it with a swipe of her tongue.

Another flex of her hips.

I place my hand over hers and slide it lower until I clear the hem of my shirt and slide it under, placing her hand on my bare stomach. Her eyes move to mine, again with that brief look of surprise followed by a widening of her eyes and her trademark enthusiastic smile.

She raises herself off of my chest enough to shove my shirt halfway up my chest, and in the same movement she spreads her legs. Spreads them so that she's straddled my right thigh. The movement causes her skirt to bunch up around her hips so the only thing separating her from my leg is her panties.

Cotton. I can feel that much under my hand. I trail my fingertip along the seam around her thigh and the edge of her panties and she shivers, then smiles, biting her lip mid-smile. It makes the skin on her nose scrunch up, the freckles from her afternoon in the sun an adorable bunch.

Another flex of her hips.

I can feel the heat of her pussy through my pants and it's fucking unreal. It's unreal because my pants are still on. What the actual fuck is happening right now? Are we... dry-humping? Is this grown woman—too young for me, yes, but grown all the same—rubbing one out on my leg?

Her lips part on a gasp, her hair a pile of tumbling strands surrounding her face. Some of it is stuck to her lips so I reach up and pull it free, tucking it behind her ear. My fingers linger, tracing the shell of her ear, down the side of her neck, across her clavicle. She smiles and grinds herself against my leg, both palms resting on my bare chest for balance.

I don't think I've dry-humped since I got my driver's license, so it's been... a while.

And yet I'm hard. Painfully hard watching her rock back and forth on my leg. Shocked my dick is still in my pants, but hard.

I drop my hands to her thighs, bare with her skirt bunched around her waist. Her skin is soft and smooth under my palms and touching her like this feels better than it should. Better than anything I've felt in a really long time.

Her eyes dart down to where my hands are stroking her skin. She must like what she sees because she licks her lips and when her eyes find mine again they're eager. Expectant and wide-eyed and the most lovely shade of green, the kind of green usually associated with a forest or an Irish festival. The shade of green reserved for men who give a fuck about noting such a detail. They're flirtatious and inquisitive and so sweetly interested in what she's looking at. Which is me.

I want to tell her not to bother. That she wouldn't like what she found if she spent more time with me. That I'm not worthy of whatever idealistic fantasy of me she's painting in her head. I want to tell her this.

I do.

I should.

I will.

But I also want to see if she can make herself come simply from rocking back and forth on my leg, or if she needs a little help.

I want to slip my hand into her cotton panties and see how wet she is. I want to know how hard her clit is. How eager and slick. I want to know if she enjoys teasing little circles made by the tip of a finger or the firm press of a thumb at just the right moment.

And God help me, I don't want her to stop looking at me like that.

She smiles and that perfect pink tongue darts out for another swipe of her lower lip. Then she bends her elbows enough to kiss me. I let her. I keep my hands on her thighs while she rocks against me again and as she presses gentle kisses against my lips. When she snakes a hand out from underneath my shirt to run her hand along the hard length of me, I let her.

I let her, when what I want to do is take control. What I want is to unzip my pants, fist myself, slide her panties to the side and slip inside of her hot, wet, tight cunt. But if I take the lead I can't watch her use me to get herself off. And that shit is hot as fuck. Hotter than is reasonable for someone my age. Or her age for that matter. Yet she's doing it for me right now with this PG-rated makeout session, so if she wants to play after-school special, I'm game. Besides, I'm far too curious to see where this goes.

NINE

LYDIA

I BEND OVER RHYS and kiss him. He smells like man and leather. Or maybe the leather I'm smelling is the couch we're currently making out on, because I'm that girl now. The girl who makes out on couches in the back office at a bar. To be honest, I feel pretty good about this life development. Anyway, he smells good and he feels good and he looks, well, he looks really, really good.

And he's so nice. Like he hasn't even tried to get my shirt off yet, which I'd totally let him do if he wanted to, but I guess he's taking this slow. I wonder if I'm supposed to take off my own shirt? That can't be right. What if I just whipped my shirt off right now and he was like, *Whoa, Lydia. I only like you a kissing amount, not a shirt-off amount?*

That would be terrible. Like the worst ever.

He really likes me a kissing amount so I don't want to blow it. I move my fingers up to his neck and kiss him again. His hands are stroking the backs of my thighs, long smooth strokes from mid-thigh to my butt, but he stops there, his fingertips trailing along the edge of my underwear where it rests against my ass. Then he slides his hands back down.

His palms feel huge on the backs of my legs, his skin warm against my skin, his fingers squeezing as he drags his hands up and down and all of it is making me crazy.

As in wet and horny and damn near out of my mind. I feel as though all the nerve endings in my body have moved to one spot and I just want to press myself against him to ease it. I'm aching with the need to be filled, to have him inside of me, so I'm making do with grinding myself against his leg. I wonder if I'm squeezing his thigh too hard?

I drop my lips to his neck and kiss him. He's got the hottest scruff ever and it abrades my cheek and the tip of my nose as I run my lips across his skin. I lick the side of his neck too, because I just have to taste him. He groans and uses one hand to pull me tighter against his leg and fists the other in my hair.

The hair-fisting almost makes me come. I'm so close. I drop my forehead to his neck and then he's whispering in my ear. I love the sound of his voice no matter what he's saying, but the low gruff whispers might be my undoing.

"Are you dirty, good girl?"

"Maybe," I reply with a shrug, because who knows really? But I think I might be dirty. If the hair-tugging is any indication, then yes. Firm yes. Sign me up for a one-way ticket to Dirtyville.

"Are you wet?"

Wait, did he really just ask that? What if I reply, "So wet, Rhys," and he has no idea what I'm talking about because what he really said was, "I'm bored, get off of me?" Logically one sounds nothing like the other but you never know, do you? Also I'm not accustomed to this kind of dirty talk. Once in college I was making out with a guy and he said he was gonna throw his dick up on my lips. That's an actual quote, I didn't misunderstand that one. I know this because I asked him to repeat himself. Which he did. Word for word. I don't know if that line had worked for him in the past but it was a no-go for me. Anyway, the point is, I have a limited skillset on the dirty talk and I don't want to blow this so I keep my head buried in his neck and rub my palms across his nipples while I wait to see how this plays out.

"I can feel you on my leg," he adds. His lips are at the soft spot behind my ear and his voice is gruff. His breath whispers against my neck and I shiver. Except—

Oh, my God. Am I making his pants wet? I'm going to die.

"Do you always get this wet, Lydia? You're soaking me right through your panties. Riding my leg like I'm your personal fucktoy. Using me to get yourself off." He tugs my hair so I have to lift my head and meet his gaze. "Aren't you?"

I'm going to melt. My breath is caught in my throat and I'm impossibly hotter and wetter and slightly humiliated and all I can think about is how damp my undies are against his leg and how freaking warm it feels there and how I need just a little something more. Just a nudge.

"Tell me, Lydia. Say it."

I can't. So I simply nod and avert my eyes as some odd sound comes out of my mouth that is half embarrassed squeak and half I-might-die-if-I-don't-get-to-come-soon groan.

"Do you know how hot you are? How insane you're driving me? How hard you're making me?"

"No." I shake my head, glancing back to meet his eyes once again. "I was hoping I was but I wasn't totally sure, you know?"

He looks at me, a hint of confusion crossing his face before he smiles as if I've amused him. I smile back because he's beautiful.

"You're a little tease, aren't you? You know exactly what you're doing to me."

Well, I can feel him pressing against my leg so I'm not totally oblivious. Also, I think this means he likes me more than a kissing amount so I grin in response.

"You love being filled with cock, don't you?" he asks but it's more of a statement than a question. My eyes flare and I can feel the blush covering my cheeks. I suck my bottom lip between my teeth for lack of anything to say to that.

"I bet you're tight as hell. You probably have to get this wet to take a dick, don't you? I bet you'd stretch so tight around my cock I'd have to fight not to come the moment I pushed inside of you."

Good God. No one has ever spoken to me like this. I sit up a bit and trail my fingers along the light path of hair from his belly button to the top of his jeans. Then I move my hand to the outline of his dick where it's trapped against his leg and stroke him. I want him inside of me. I feel... empty. There's no other way to explain it. I'm empty and aching to be filled with him.

He exhales on a groan when I touch him and it sounds like heaven. The low timber of sound, not even a word. His hands have moved to the tops of my legs now that I'm sitting up again. His thumbs are on the insides of my thighs, his palms on top, and he's repeating the stroking motion he was making on the backs of my legs. My skirt is bunched around my waist, allowing his hands to slide all the way up, his thumbs resting on the taut muscles of my inner thigh where I'm stretched across his own leg. His hands stop, his thumbs kneading my heated skin before brushing along the elastic seam of the crotch of my panties. I know the fabric between is wet. I can imagine how my damp curls look, the wet fabric clinging and transparent. Pale pink stripes. That's the pair I put on today when I got out of the shower after the pool. A pale pink pair of cotton high-legged briefs with thin white stripes. Anything other than plain white I'd always considered kinda sexy. I can't imagine it stacks up against the skimpy thongs made of lace and silk he must be used to seeing a woman wear.

His eyes are trained on the wet spot between my legs when he speaks. "Do you want me to make you come, Lydia?"

"I might die if you don't." I blurt the response out without thought and my pussy flutters in expectation as he smiles again like I'm amusing him in some way. He uses one thumb to hook my panties to the side and rubs the other through the triangle of hair exposed from the movement. I keep my eyes on his face while his are on the needy spot between my legs.

He slides his thumb across my slick flesh then sweeps it across my clit and—oh, God. Feeling his hands on me, watching his face as he touches me, it's intoxicating. It makes me want more. More of him, more of whatever he can do. More of his filthy words and wicked fingers. More, more, more. Then he presses his thumb firmly against my clit and I come. I don't think it even takes a full three seconds of pressure and if I was in any kind of control over myself I'd have held out longer because the feel of him touching me there is unlike anything I've ever experienced. I've had boys shove their hands down

71

my pants before, hesitant touches and groping fingers, and it didn't do much for me.

This is not like that.

Nothing like that.

He doesn't stop and the orgasm carries on in a way I'm not familiar with from giving them to myself. I'm used to a quick burst of release that has me pulling my hand away as soon as it's hit. Rhys keeps his thumb in place, rubbing firmly back and forth across the wet nub even though I'm clutching at his forearms and squirming. It's too much and I want to wiggle away. I want to stay. I want the pulsing fluttering heaven to stop. I want it never to end. My head drops forward, while a repeat of "oh, oh, oh," falls from my lips.

When it's over I collapse against his chest, snuggled under his chin while my chest rises and falls and my breathing returns to normal. Rhys whispers into my ear, words of how beautiful I am when I come, how much he enjoyed watching me. It gives me an odd sense of pride for having pleased him.

"You're really good at that, huh?" I mumble into his neck. He definitely smells good, I decide. It's not just the couch. He smells like an autumn day in Tennessee. Crisp and clean and earthy and male.

His chest moves as he laughs, his breath warming the top of my head. "Good at what exactly? I barely touched you."

"Good at thumbs, I guess. I don't know," I murmur into his neck again because I'm busy trailing my fingers along his skin, the pads of my fingertips occupied with committing the feel of his scruff to memory. The clean shave line, the smooth skin beneath it. The muscles of his neck. I find everything about him really, really interesting.

"Where the hell did you come from?" he says while winding a strand of my hair through his fingers.

"Knoxville." I sit up and look at him. "Tennessee," I add when he just stares at me. It takes me another few seconds to realize the question was rhetorical and then I feel stupid so I ask him where he came from. It doesn't make it any better, but it's all I could come up with.

"Connecticut," he replies, because my question was not rhetorical. A small frown mars his forehead as he examines my face. Then he wipes the thumb he just got me off with across his tongue, his eyes not leaving mine. I suck in a breath, because wow. And now I'm wondering what he's thinking. What I taste like. If he liked it. I'm also reminded that only one of us got off.

"You're still hard," I say, stroking the length of him over his jeans. He really is. Hard. And big. I squeeze him gently through the denim.

"Who wouldn't be?" he replies on a long hiss of an exhale.

I glance at him, not sure what that means. Does it mean I'm some kind of sexual temptress capable of making any man rock-hard? Hmm, that would be pretty cool if that was true. Or does it mean I've just gotten off while he's gotten nothing and I should do something to fix it?

"Do you, um, want to?" Yeah, that came out well. I'm not even sure what I just offered. A hand job? Sex? Who knows? Why the heck isn't he taking charge? In my fantasy vision of this he tells me what to do so I don't have to bumble my way through it. He says stuff like, "Lydia, I want to fuck you. Let's go back to my place and do the fucking." I mean, obviously it sounds better when he says it—I told you my dirty-talking skills need work.

"Do I want to what?" He's looking at me under hooded eyes, his voice low and sexy as all heck. His gaze drops to my lips before returning to my eyes and it feels like a caress, the way he looks at me. It feels like he's smoothing a palm against my cheek and pulling me closer to him instead of simply running his eyes across my face. "Do I want to fuck? Do I want to alleviate this hard-on you've given me? Do I want to find out just how tight your pussy is? How slick and hot? Do I want to finger you to see if you're ready to fuck right this second, or if you'll need a second finger and some stretching before I can get inside of you? Do I want to know what your orgasm feels like fluttering against my cock while I'm buried balls deep inside of you?"

He pauses.

"Who wouldn't want that, Lydia?"

Whew. Okay, so same page then.

"Or maybe I'd like to try that pretty mouth first. I'd expect you to take it all, though. I'd squeeze your jaw open with one hand and feed you my cock with the other until you gagged. Then I'd slide it down your throat while you choked on me. Would that be okay with you, Lydia? Do you give sweet blow jobs with your pretty lips wrapped around nothing more than the tip? Or do you take it until your nose is pressed against a man's stomach and your next breath is reliant on him letting you up?"

Oh.

Well.

He'd have to teach me that bit, obviously.

"Not here, right?" I glance at the door and then

back to Rhys. He can't mean to do all that here, in a bar office where anyone could walk in. And this couch isn't mine, or his even. What if it's messy? What if I... bleed on it? I feel myself flush in embarrassment and I suck my bottom lip between my teeth.

"Why not here?"

Um. Because. "Because." I shrug one shoulder and glance at the door again. *Because I don't want to get deflowered on a couch in a bar, Rhys.* Which reminds me that I'm still working on a better word than deflowering. Devirginating? I wonder if that's a real word or an Urban Dictionary word. "My place is close," I offer in what I hope is a helpful tone, deciding that this isn't the time or place to blurt out, *I'm still a virgin, would you mind terribly divesting me of that?*

He lifts a brow at my response. "Do you only fuck in beds, good girl? You're twenty-two, surely you've fucked in a back seat a time or two?"

"You want to go out to the parking lot?" He can't be serious, can he? I can't hide the surprise in my voice and I'm sure the expression on my face matches because he laughs.

"You're sweet. And this isn't happening."

And then he dumps me off his lap and walks out the door.

TEN

LYDIA

"'THIS ISN'T HAPPENING?'" I'm pacing the kitchen floor and repeating myself. "'This isn't happening' is even worse than 'whatever else you want!'"

"Great. So you're even now on saying stupid things." Payton takes a drag on the milkshake she made us stop to get on the way home. To be fair, we got it in the drive-thru at Del Taco so it wasn't a big detour. Also, I stress-ate an entire Queso Crunch Taco Meal before we made it back to the apartment so I've no room to complain about the stop.

"What is with him and his mixed message bullshit?" I wave my arms about before slumping over the table in exasperation.

"Oh, wow. You're unpacking the swear words now. Whoa," Payton murmurs with brows raised. "Shit's getting serious."

"See, this is how I'm still a virgin! Men are so freaking complicated. And stupid. I hate them. All of them."

"Are you going lesbian on me right now? Listen, I respect your choices, yadda yadda, but I don't think I'm into you like that. If you're asking. But maybe in a three-way sister-wife situation? I would share a penis with you for sure. That might work."

"What?" I blink at her a few times. "Are you hitting on me?"

"No." She shakes her head, her expression nonplussed as if this is all perfectly clear. "I was offering to share a man with you. Theoretically. If it came to that," she adds with a shrug. "Which is a very generous offer. You should be a little more appreciative."

"What?" I repeat again, slowly. Has she lost her mind? "How would that even work?"

"Like a timeshare. I'd get him on Mondays, Wednesdays and Fridays. And then you'd get him on Tuesdays, Thursdays and Saturdays!" She takes another slurp of milkshake and looks at me expectantly, as if I might have some feedback on this theoretical boyfriend timeshare. "It was nice of me to offer you the Saturday spot, wasn't it?" She looks at me again, head tilted to the side, milkshake in hand.

"Right," I respond even though nothing about that sounded right. "And what would happen on Sundays? He'd get to pick up random women on Sundays?"

"No! Don't be gross." Payton shoots me a dirty look, as if I've offended her by even thinking it. "He doesn't get to pick up random women, ever. He's totally faithful to us. Sundays would be for threesomes. Or he could have the day off. Whatever."

I stare at her for several seconds without speaking as I process that.

"Move." I wave at the seat she's in. "I need the table to make sheet pajamas." I grab a pincushion and a half-finished pair of pants and sit. "Um, thank you for the generous offer. I'll keep that idea on the back burner."

"Anytime. I'm a really good friend."

"That you are. And so modest."

"And a good sharer. Don't forget that part. You know I really think the sister-wife lifestyle is underutilized."

"Uh-huh."

"Like, imagine if Chris Hemsworth was into both of us and wanted to marry both of us."

"Chris Hemsworth is already married."

"Lydia." Payton groans my name on a long sigh. "Don't be so literal. Imagine we bump into a single Chris Hemsworth."

"Okay."

"And imagine he's even greater than you'd imagined. Hotter, nicer, better in bed."

"Uh-huh."

"And then imagine he wanted both of us. That he wanted to marry both of us and buy side-by-side houses for us where we'd raise our plethora of children together. Who would say no to that? Who?" she repeats, eyes wide and palms up, her expression telling me that she cannot imagine how anyone could say no.

"I think most women would say no to that."

"Well, that's dumb." She drops her hands and waves dismissively. "I'd say yes. Hopefully my sister-wife would be more open-minded than you are."

"One can only hope."

"It would also be great if she enjoyed cooking, because I don't. She could do the cooking and I'd do the laundry. Honestly don't understand how this is not a thing," she mutters to herself.

"Isn't it a little sexist that you're assuming the cooking and laundry falls to you and your sister-wife? Wouldn't your perfect version of Chris

Hemsworth also cook, clean and do the laundry?"

"Ohhh, good call." Payton looks genuinely interested for a moment then shakes her head. "Except in my fantasy version the guy is very busy running his billionaire app empire, so I'm not sure he'd have the time to do the cooking, cleaning, run his business and keep two women sexually satisfied."

"I thought your fantasy was Chris Hemsworth."

"It was, but I moved on when we established that he's already married. Do you have any scraps?" she asks, nodding towards my pile of cut-up sheets. Apparently she's moved on from worrying about how the household chores will be divided in her fictional future.

"Sure." I nod absently towards the pieces I'm done with. Payton pops out of her chair and then returns with a handful of Sharpies. I mostly ignore her because I'm still thinking about Rhys and how I managed to lose him mere minutes after I came. On his freaking hand. One minute we're negotiating where I'm going to choke on his cock, the next minute he's shoving me off his lap and walking out the door.

I'm so confused.

Obviously I don't know him that well, but he seems like a reasonable enough person, so I can't imagine he left simply because I didn't want to have sex on a couch. It's not as though I was saying no to couch sex forever, just no to couch sex right at that moment, on that couch, in that office. Maybe he's really into the height of couches? Or he wanted me to bend over the back of it? I don't know. But I'm totally open to the future potential of couches.

I'd have made that clearer if he'd stayed long enough to talk about it. Jerk.

I'm almost certain I'm a firm no on the back seat of a car though. I'm too old for that, aren't I? I think that ship has sailed. I have my own apartment—well, almost my own apartment. I have my own room so I cannot envision any reasonable need to have sex in a car. Plus I don't have a garage and Rhys probably parks in the parking garage at the Windsor so, like, where would we even do it?

He was probably just making a point with the back seat comment anyway.

He thinks I'm too good for him. And not in a 'I'm a nice person' way. But in a 'sexually incompatible' way. Which is really really unfair, because I'm positive we're very sexually compatible. Granted I've never had sex before and have no idea what I'm talking about, but I can feel it. I know we'd be good together, I just know it. Lust is a very real and tangible thing, as it turns out. That must be the reason I lose my mind around him. Lust. Because it's not as if I haven't had access to men before I laid eyes on him. I haven't been in a convent. Or a coma. I've even dated a little.

But no one has made me feel the way Rhys does.

No one has ever caused me to offer myself up carte blanche before. Honestly, keeping my panties on until this point hasn't been much of a challenge. Before I laid eyes on Rhys, that is. It wasn't until seeing him that I turned into a total slut. A sad wannabe slut with a dirty imagination and an aversion to losing her virginity on a couch.

Fail.

"Scissors," Payton demands, pulling me from my self-pity by holding out her hand as if she's in surgery and requesting a scalpel. I sigh, put down my pincushion and make a big show of placing the scissors in her palm. Then I watch as she sets down her Sharpie and carefully begins cutting.

"What are you doing?"

"Making you a badge."

"Um." I try to get a better look but I can't make sense of it as she rotates the fabric and continues to snip. "Okay," I say for lack of anything better.

"Done!" Payton sets the scissors down then picks it up and slaps it down on the table in front of me, a huge smile covering her face. She appears to be genuinely proud over her creation.

She's drawn a foaming glass of beer onto a heart-shaped piece of scrap sheet fabric. I glance at it and then back to her.

"What is this?"

"A bar badge!" she announces with, yes, I'm going with pride.

"You made me a badge. For a bar." I run my fingers along it. I have to admit she's done nice work. "A heart-shaped badge. What level uses heart-shaped badges?" I'm joking because heart-shaped badges do not exist.

"The fun level."

I frown at her, suspicious. "What did I do to earn this badge?"

"You had an orgasm in a bar." She says this part as if she assumed the criteria for the bar badge were obvious.

"You are so messed up," I mutter.

"They didn't kick me out of the Girl Troopers for nothing. Now, we need a sash. Let's see what we can use." She jumps up and starts digging through my pile of sheet fabric.

"Whoa, what do you mean we need a sash?"

"For your badge?" she replies, again with a frown

as if I'm simply not getting it. "Where are we supposed to display all your badges if you don't have a sash?"

"All what badges?"

"All the fun badges you're going to earn," she says without looking at me as she digs a faded floral print from the pile. "Can I use this?"

Okay, the thing is, I really do enjoy earning badges. I find it very satisfying.

"What other badges do you have in mind?" I try to ask it casually, like it's a joke, but I'm not sure how successful I am. I twirl a lock of hair around my fingertip and try to look nonchalant. It's been so long since I had a new badge to earn.

"The next badge is the 'no fucks' badge."

"Haven't I already earned that badge? By not having sex?"

"It's more of a 'fuck everyone' badge." Payton spreads the fabric across my cutting mat and picks up the acrylic cutting ruler, lining it up neatly along the edge of the fabric.

"Payton, I told you group sex is not my thing. Normally I believe in trying something before you decide it's not for you, but I just don't think sex parties are something one tries unless they have a predisposed interest."

"Um, wow." She's bent over the fabric smoothing the wrinkles with her hand but she stops and stands up straight. "You are really literal." She hands me the cutting ruler and motions to my chair. "Switch places with me."

"I thought you were making me a sash."

"I was, but then I realized sewing is pretty complicated and I want to do a good job so I think you should do it."

"I should make the sash because you want to do a good job," I repeat as I stand and switch places with her. "So many things are making sense right now."

"Make sure you do a good job because I have pride in my work."

"Of course you do." I realign the fabric on the cutting mat then place the ruler and make a quick swipe through the fabric with the rotary cutter, before moving the ruler and making a second cut so that I have five inch-wide strips of fabric. Then I grab my pincushion and start pinning the strips together so I can make a hidden seam.

"Anyway, we'll call your next badge the confidence badge," Payton says as she gets to work with her Sharpies. "Since calling it the 'fuck everyone' badge seems a little dicey for you. You haven't earned this one yet, but I'm going to make it and hang it on the fridge so you have a goal."

"Do you think this is a bit dysfunctional?"

"No. I think this is adulting done right."

I do like having goals so I decide she must be correct.

ELEVEN

LYDIA

IT TURNS OUT I can earn the confidence badge by going to work on Monday. It's a little more complicated than that, but that's the gist. Payton said new week, new me. She said I have to go be brave, go to work, and not fire myself.

She also said that since Rhys made out with me it means she was right that propositioning him for sex made his day. I reminded her that he turned me down for sex and she insisted it was because he has an erectile dysfunction. She's a really sweet friend to say so, but I don't think it's true. I think he rejected me because he didn't want to have sex with me. Which is his right, obviously. Absolutely.

Payton said Rhys needs to stop kissing me if he's not going to put out. I told her that gender equality works both ways and it's offensive for her to imply that a man is a tease for wanting to stop at kissing. I don't think I got through to her though because she fell asleep while I was talking. She had a Cheez-It in one hand and was splayed across the sofa like the errant toddlers I used to babysit in high school. I took the Cheez-It from her and covered her with a blanket before taking myself to bed where I lay awake for a long time, thinking about Rhys. Thinking about my reaction to him. Thinking about my feelings. Thinking, thinking, thinking.

I head into Monday more confident than I did exiting Friday, though.

A bit.

Enough to agree that it's not likely I'll get fired, but not enough to have a clue about what I'm supposed to do about Rhys. I really don't understand why he's so determined to avoid me. I felt how much he liked me on Saturday—literally, I felt it on my leg. So what's the problem? I'm not asking for him to marry me and father my children, for crying out loud.

Unless.

Shit.

Maybe that's it? Maybe he's tired of women using him for sex. It must happen a lot—looking at him, I can see how it would. I can't be the only girl who loses her mind at the sight of him. I bet he's sick of women treating him like a sex object. Especially when he has so much more to offer. Like, he probably does all sorts of things other than have sex. Like he might golf and... I'm drawing a blank about what else he might be interested in. Because I am a terrible person using him for sex. Ugh, no wonder he nearly shoved me off of him and left the bar.

But I like the way he kisses me. And I know that should fall under a sexual thing, and it does. But it also falls under something I simply just like about him. Something that showed me who he is when he's with me. I liked how he held me that first time he kissed me. The way his hand felt on my hip and the way he didn't push me for more or slide his hands to places that might have startled me in the moment.

The way that it felt like he respected me, even though I was a stranger he was kissing in a bar. I liked it that he took me into the back office instead of kissing me in front of everyone the way a lot of men might have.

And the second time—well, I liked everything about that. The twitch in his jaw when he stood in front of me as I was playing darts with Josh. The possessive way he took my hand in his and walked us in back. Maybe I should have been irritated by that—and I suppose if I was interested in Josh I might have been annoyed. But I wasn't annoyed, I was thrilled. Thrilled to see Rhys again. Thrilled to have my hand tucked in his. Thrilled to have him to myself.

I liked the way he arranged us on the sofa so that I wasn't trapped underneath him. I liked the way he looked at me, like he was fascinated by me, like he wanted to devour me, like I was beautiful. I liked the way he laughed at me, his expression relaxing, the tiny lines by his eyes creasing from a lifetime of repetition. I like, I like, I like.

But are those all sexual things? Are all those likes me objectifying him? I decide I should work on finding more things that I like about him. Things that have nothing to do with touching and sex and feelings. Like respecting him for who he is as a person.

Good plan.

I mentally pat myself on the back as the elevator opens onto the fourth floor and I make my way to my desk. I call hello to my new co-workers as I pass and decide this is going to be a great week. Heck, I've already earned a new badge just for walking in the door today and I know Payton is working on more of them.

I am momentarily flummoxed by the dirty coffee cup I was forced to leave on my desk as I fled the building on Friday, but I refuse to be waylaid by a mug. Nope. Not happening. So I set my things down and take the offending cup to the break room. I wash it thoroughly and then place it in the dishwasher for good measure. Grabbing a clean cup, I use the fancy coffee machine to make a latte. See! This day is already going better than Friday, since I'm able to pay attention to the machine and I actually know what I'll be drinking.

I wonder if Rhys likes coffee? I've only seen him drink water and a beer, that first time at the bar. He drinks water really nicely though, so that's something besides sex and his face that I like him for. Another check mark in the win column for today.

Except, shit. Is it? Because it sorta turned me on—watching him take a sip of water. But does that count as something I like about him or does that count as objectifying him?

I suspect everything that I learn about him will turn me on though, so I'm not sure I can separate the things I like about him from the things that turn me on. Like if I learned that he calls his mom every Sunday that would both turn me on and be something that I liked about him.

This is oddly complicated.

I decide I'll ask Payton later how she differentiates things she likes about a man versus the things she finds sexually attractive about him.

Back at my desk I settle into my workweek, checking emails and double-checking my meeting calendar. The grand opening is in three weeks, which means new hire processing and orientations begin in earnest today for the front-of-house staff.

Housekeeping, bell services, dealers, food services, front desk, recreation and on and on and on. The majority of the hiring is done, the interview process and background checks complete. The new hire paperwork, not so much. My life for the next month will be nothing but orientations, training and paperwork.

I'm giddy at the very thought.

You know how some kids play grocery store? With their little plastic cash registers and pretend money? Forcing their parents to purchase plastic oranges and empty cartons of cereal so they can bag up the order and make change for a fake twenty-dollar bill?

I wasn't that kid.

I think it was the cookies. I never needed to play store because I got to do the real thing selling cookies. The real fun for me was the forms. I loved the paperwork. I loved calculating how many more boxes I needed to sell to reach my goal. I loved ensuring all the orders were fulfilled correctly and making a sweep of highlighter across the order form as each order was delivered. I loved that part.

So I'm thrilled to get the day underway. Thrilled when I open my schedule and realize I've been assigned policy training. I really wasn't paying attention on Friday, was I? I love policies. Policies are my jam!

This is going to be the best week ever.

TWELVE

LYDIA

IT WASN'T THE BEST week ever. It wasn't the worst either, it was just meh. I was anxious about bumping into Rhys. Scared I would, terrified I wouldn't. Butterflies in my stomach every time I thought I might. Constantly on the lookout for him, like a lovesick teenager hoping to get a glimpse of the homecoming king in the halls between classes. Dumb. It was torture. Agony.

Pathetic.

I saw him four times. He ignored me all four. Well, to be fair he only saw me twice. I don't think he even noticed me the other two times. As I said, pathetic. I should give up. As if this man is thinking twice about me during what presumably must be the biggest moment of his career—getting this resort opened. As if he'd think twice about me even on a random Tuesday.

So I do my job. I conduct orientation after orientation after orientation. I answer endless questions about insurance plans and benefit packages and the correct number of deductions to claim on a W-4. I steal glances at Rhys every chance I get and file away everything I learn about him. He looks good in striped ties. And solid ones. He drinks the espresso from the fancy coffee machine in the break room. He makes me wet and needy just being within twenty feet of him. I guess that last one wasn't really a revelation.

Outside of work I make myself familiar with half a dozen Goodwill stores and their ever-rotating stock of old sheets. Payton surprises me by arriving home one evening with a Jo-Ann Fabrics bag stuffed full of felt and sequins and buttons and glitter pens. She's taken to badge-making with a passion greater than I'd have thought possible, and with enviable skill. Which is how I end up on a dating app talking to guys I don't really want to talk to. But Rhys doesn't want to talk to me either, so I might as well earn the dating app badge, am I right? It's a really nice badge too. Payton went all out with the glitter pen and some buttons, and all I had to do to earn it was install the app on my phone and open the messages.

Which I have, and survey says, I'm never going to lose my virginity. Honestly, I thought virgins were in higher demand than this. If I'd known it was going to be so hard to get rid of I'd just have given it to Mark Novak after prom because I'm beginning to feel like a carton of soon-to-expire milk. The one that people dig past to find a better carton, or just leave on the shelf altogether in favor of the fancier, sluttier milk, almond.

On the plus side, I've decided if I ever become a stripper my stripper name will be Almond. It's good to have backup plans and strippers never use their real names so I think this revelation was one well worth having. And I could use Ally for short when I want something a bit more playful. Almond for the serious customers with commitment issues.

I wonder if Rhys even knows what a dating app is? I decide he probably doesn't. He doesn't look like a guy who would need to swipe left, right, up or down to get a date. Which makes the fact that I offered myself to him on a silver platter all the more frustrating. Or maybe it should make it less frustrating? It should make it less, I suppose. If he was desperate to get laid and still didn't want to have sex with me that would be way worse than him having endless options and not wanting to have sex with me. Somehow this does nothing to make me feel better.

I do my best to test the theory that I'm mistakenly enamored with Rhys and could want someone else just as easily. It's never happened before, but maybe I haven't tried hard enough? So I try. I keep an open mind on that dating app. I open the messages I'm sent. I read them. I think about replying. When Josh—I remember his name now—when Josh asks if he can take me out for dinner I don't say no. I don't say yes, either. I dodge the invite with a 'maybe next weekend,' because I don't know, maybe? Maybe I'll snap out of this spell I'm under. Maybe my heart will stop beating faster whenever Rhys is nearby. Maybe I'll stop creating imaginary scenarios where Rhys and I are alone in an elevator. Maybe, maybe, maybe.

Maybe not.

I want Rhys. And he must want me at least a little. He did make me come, after all. I can't imagine men make women come if they're not at least a little interested. Plus one of the times he saw me his gaze lingered on my lips. I think. I can't exactly be trusted when it comes to Rhys so I can't be certain but I'm pretty sure it happened.

"I NEED A RHYS badge," I declare as I set my lunch down and slide into a seat next to Payton in the employee cafeteria. It's been two weeks since he rolled me off his lap and left me with the parting words that we weren't happening. I still think we are.

"Are you really sure that's what you need?" Payton answers, fiddling with a straw wrapper and avoiding my eyes.

"Well, what I need is a plan, and positive reinforcements have always done wonders to motivate me. Why do you think I sold so many freaking cookies?"

"Because you're a goody two-shoes?"

"Yes," I agree, pointing at her with my fork, "that is true. But I find the badge reward system very satisfying and I'm sure once you make a Rhys badge, a plan will come to me." I smile and fork a heap of mashed potatoes into my mouth.

It's a comfort food kind of day. It's been a crazy two weeks. We had our soft opening this week, meaning the doors opened and the first guests have checked in, but it's mostly journalists and travel industry executives with comped rooms. It's allowed the staff to get their feet wet before the official grand opening in two weeks. We're already booked to ninety percent capacity for that week, so they don't have much time to get their routines down and work out any kinks.

"There's something I have to tell you," Payton says, and it turns out I've got some kinks to work out too.

THIRTEEN

LYDIA

"SO HE LIKES TO pay for it? Is that what I'm dealing with here?" Lord, he's really not making this easy on me. I know they say nothing worth having comes easily, but this is asking a lot out of a virgin. Yet... I'm strangely attracted to the idea. But is that fucked up? Being turned on by the idea of him paying me for it?

Probably.

But I am.

Imagining Rhys picking me, it makes me warm, makes me flush in places I shouldn't. The idea that I could control the experience. The when and where. The idea that I'd turn myself over to Rhys, let him spread my legs and fuck me, without even taking me to dinner first... it turns me on.

It's so backwards. Upside-down and confusing and wrong. But it removes the doubt, doesn't it? If he picks me, if he pays for me, he wants me. And that is thrilling and freeing and liberating in ways I wouldn't have thought. I won't have to question if he's interested. If I'm his type, if he's sexually attracted to me. If my boobs are too small or my inexperience too off-putting.

Maybe my lust is making me delusional, but it makes sense to me. It's just so oddly clear-cut this way. It feels right to me, it turns me on, and that's all that really matters, isn't it?

"He loves paying for it. Allegedly. Per my source," Payton says, dropping her voice to a conspiratorial whisper even though we're alone.

"Your source is a bellhop who swipes his keycard so the girls can access the elevator to the executive floor."

"I confirmed the story with my new friend in housekeeping!" Payton's done speaking softly, clearly outraged by my assessment of her intel. "I didn't bring this story to you without confirmation. This isn't Watergate."

"Nope." I shake my head. "I agree, this is nothing like Watergate. Not even a tiny bit."

Payton nods smugly as she takes a bite of her lunch and while I think.

I spend the rest of lunch lost in thought—the rest of the day, if I'm being honest. Then I hatch a plan. A completely crazy plan.

"ARE YOU ABSOLUTELY sure you want to do this?" Payton asks for possibly the third time since last night. "Or that this idea you have is even feasible? Maybe you could try propositioning him again first? It seems like that would be a lot easier. And saner. I feel like we might be getting a little carried away here with this plan of yours."

"Possibly. But I'm a very goal-oriented person and I want to lose my virginity this century. Preferably to

Rhys. There's definitely chemistry between us, and he's clearly on the licentious side so he's either rejecting me because he's got some kind of fetish for paying for it or some hangup I haven't figured out yet. Or he thinks I'm too much of a good girl to be interested in what he's interested in." Spoiler, Rhys, I'm not that good.

Also, I read a romance novel once about a virgin auction and it ended in a happily-ever-after. But I keep that to myself because it's too crazytown to say out loud, even to Payton.

Payton plucks her Del Taco cup from the cup holder in my car and takes a sip. Their java iced coffees are life-affirming, and the value size is only a buck and less than a hundred and fifty calories so I can have one without fat or financial guilt. Plus, we deserved the caffeine this morning because we're on our way to Double Diamonds, which is reported to be a frequent club of choice for Rhys.

"Are you sure this place is open before noon on a Saturday?" I ask again, because why would a strip club be open before lunch? I'm in no position to judge anyone's life choices but I'm having trouble visualizing a scenario where one would need a lap dance before noon. Which is precisely why we're going this early, so we won't accidentally bump into Rhys before I'm ready.

"Twenty-four hours. I checked their website."

"They have a website?"

"Who doesn't have a website?"

Hmm. "Should I have applied online, do you think?"

Payton chokes on her iced coffee before setting it back in the cup holder. "No, I don't think you should have applied to be a prostitute online. I think that's an in-person kind of application."

"Okay."

"Besides which, their website is just for the dancers. I think the hookers are all very hush-hush."

"That sounds right."

"Totally."

"You know what I don't get though?"

"What?"

"Can't he find women willing to have sex with him for free? Clearly I would. Look at him."

"Well, you know what they say."

"What do they say?"

"Men like that, they're not paying for sex. They're paying for her to leave after."

Wow. That's really sad.

"You know he's gonna want anal, right?" Payton adds.

"I assumed so," I reply with a shrug.

"Don't worry," Payton says breezily. "I'm gonna make you a 'butt stuff' badge."

"You're a good friend."

"I really am," Payton agrees, rattling the ice in her drink.

WHEN WE ARRIVE AT Double Diamonds and step inside it's not what I expected, not at all. It's as awkward as I'd expected, two women walking into a strip club before noon. We're immediately asked if we'd like applications.

"I'd like to speak to the owner," I reply, doing my best to sound confident.

"Me too," Payton adds and I give her the side eye

because I'm not sure if she's supporting me or if she actually wants an application.

It's my lucky day because it turns out that the owner, Vince, is here. And he's willing to give us fifteen minutes.

As we're escorted through the club to Vince's office, I take in my surroundings. I expected it to be dark with an elevated stage in the center of the room outlined with neon lighting. There is a stage, of course. There are three of them, each smaller than I'd envisioned in my mind. The chairs are so much closer to the stages than I'd imagined too. Overall the place feels more like a buffalo wing bar than a house of ill repute. If buffalo wing bars had poles, obviously. There's a pretty blonde dancing for a man sitting alone. He's drinking coffee, his eyes never leaving her body as we pass. I wonder what brought him to a strip club by himself before lunch, but seeing that I'm here for my own nefarious reasons I'm in no position to judge.

Once we're seated in Vince's office, Payton breaks the ice with her signature chitchat while my heart races a million miles an hour. I focus on my surroundings and take a deep breath while I summon the courage to ask what I want to ask. The office has an oddly comforting vibe. Safe. There's not a neon light to be had or needed, as natural sunlight streams in from the oversized windows lining an entire wall. The office décor is nondescript corporate. I'd think I'd just wandered into a law office, if law offices had lobbies with poles in them.

"So, do you have multiple girlfriends?" Payton dives right in with her own agenda after we've been offered coffee by a woman who's got to be in her sixties. I fleetingly wonder if they advertised for that position on a job board or if they promoted her from within.

"Excuse me?" Vince replies, eyebrows raised in question, clearly confused if he's misheard Payton or simply misjudged the audacity she's capable of.

"You know, like Hugh Hefner did?"

"I run a gentleman's club in Vegas, not a lifestyle magazine."

"Same thing. Anyway, do you? Because Rhys is gonna fall in love with Lydia and they'll move in together and yadda yadda yadda. I'll have to get a new roommate and I'm not sure I can be bothered to vet someone new right now. So I'd be open to being girlfriend number three. I don't want to be girlfriend one or two, it sounds like too much responsibility, you know? Also I'd like my own room. Is that how you do it? Do the girlfriends all get their own rooms? That's how Hef did it. Do you have a nice place? Because I'm not sharing you if you live in a shitty condo with coin-operated laundry."

"Are you serious?" Vince narrows his eyes at her, as if he can't tell if Payton is indeed serious or simply fucking with him, and Vince doesn't look like a man used to being fucked with. I find most people have this reaction to her, so I'm used to it. For the record, she's rarely joking when she's saying something ridiculous.

"Serious as a shark," she replies without blinking.

"That's not even a thing." Vince brings a cup of coffee to his lips, eyeing her over the rim. "The saying is 'serious as a heart attack.'"

"Like sharks aren't serious?" She leans forward, her eyes narrowed. "You try swimming with a shark and then tell me how not-serious they are."

"You know he slept with all of them, right?"

"Duh," Payton replies, completely nonplussed about the sleeping arrangements of a man and his multiple girlfriends.

"You're really something, aren't you?" Vince asks, still looking at her as if he's not sure what to make of her.

"I'm a lot of things. It's true." Payton beams as if he's just paid her a compliment. I'm honestly not sure what his feelings are about her because his expression isn't giving away much. But if I had to guess, he's not inviting Payton to be girlfriend number one, two or three anytime soon.

"Vince," I say, squaring my shoulders and interrupting before Payton gets us kicked out. I take a deep breath. I can do this. I can, I can, I can. "I have a proposition for you."

He takes his eyes off of Payton and levels me with the full force of his attention and I have a fleeting worry about who exactly I'm dealing with. He could be a mobster, couldn't he? He owns a strip club—gentleman's club, whatever—in the heart of Las Vegas. He might have ties to organized crime. Or loan sharks or hitmen. I don't know this man or what he's involved in. I doubt he's leading a church youth group on the weekends, I assume that much. And I'm sure he's not someone to mess with. Not that I'm messing with him, I'm not. I'm serious. But it doesn't mean I'm not in way over my head.

"I'm listening, Miss Clark," he says, his eyes flickering to his desktop monitor and back to mine. "You've got nine minutes left. If you want something you'd better get to it. Quickly."

So I blurt out my request because I've got nothing to lose. Because I'm not a quitter. Because I've got a plan.

There's a moment of silence when I'm done. A long moment. Vince stares at me, silent, his fingers drumming on his desktop. Payton takes a drag on her iced coffee, but there's nothing left in the cup so the room fills with that rattling hollow noise that occurs from creating a wind tunnel in an empty cup. She rattles the ice as if that might get her an extra drop or two and slurps again.

"Are you for real?" Vince stops staring at me to address Payton.

"So real. And so are my boobs."

His eyes drop slowly to her chest before he shakes his head and returns his attention to me. "This isn't a brothel," he says, and I'm afraid he's about to boot me from his office, my time long gone. "Prostitution isn't legal in Clark County."

"Of course not. Double Diamonds is a business, isn't it, Mr...?"

"Vince," he replies, deadpan.

"Right. Mr. Vince, you're a businessman at heart, aren't you? So let's make a deal. I'll make it worth your while, I promise."

"Scout's honor," Payton adds and as I turn to look at her she winks at him, a big dramatic wink complete with a head tilt and a little tsk she makes with her tongue. "The Urban Dictionary kind, big guy."

I don't even want to know what that means, so I shoot her a look meant to make her shut up and turn back to Vince.

He leans back in his chair, running two fingers across his lips while he watches us with newfound interest. "So you work at the Windsor. Both of you?"

I nod, feeling like I might be on the verge of changing his mind.

"Let's talk terms."

FOURTEEN

"ARE YOU GOING TO introduce your girlfriend to your parents when they're in for the grand opening?" Canon asks as he strolls into my suite as if he's got all the time in the world for socializing. He drops onto a chair across from the sofa I'm sitting on and raises his eyebrows as if in expectation of a real answer.

"Fuck off, Canon."

"The fact that you're not even questioning who I'm referring to is sad."

"I'm busy here, Canon," I tell him, nodding at my laptop. "I don't have the time or interest to address the bullshit that comes from your mouth on a good day, let alone at present. And if you would stop using the master key to walk into my place of residence I'd appreciate it."

"Why don't you just grow up and ask her on a date?" he asks, ignoring my dig at his free usage of my front door.

"Wait." I give up on the reports in front of me and give Canon my full attention. "Are you advising me on my life choices right now? You had a threesome with two strippers last night."

"Yeah, and whose fault was that? One of them was

for you but you claimed you were too busy to get laid. What was I supposed to do with her? Send her home unlaid?"

"Do what with whom?" Lawson strolls into my suite as if he too has nothing but time.

"What is this? Are we having a party? Do neither of you have anything to do? Our grand opening is in"—I check my watch—"two weeks."

"I've got jack shit to do." Lawson runs a hand through his hair, leaving it in disarray. "It'll be at least two weeks and a day before the first frivolous lawsuit rolls in. Also, it's Saturday, you dick," he adds with a grin. "Live a little." I'm about to tell him I'll live once the grand opening is behind us and to get the hell out of my place but he's already ignoring me, having dropped into the chair next to Canon.

"I'm good too," Canon says. "But thanks." He angles his phone in Lawson's direction. "The giraffes or elephants?"

"The giraffes." Lawson stretches as if he's getting comfortable to stay a while, his legs sprawled out, completely at ease, and grabs the remote from my coffee table.

"Agreed. Do you want to go in with me on a stroller? Shit, these things are pricey," Canon murmurs while tapping on the screen of his phone.

"Sure. But order a Bugaboo though, I'm not going in on a shitty umbrella stroller."

"What are you guys doing?" I stop working—again—to pay better attention to Canon and Lawson, my eyes narrowing as I remind myself of the lengths Canon will go to to amuse himself.

"Making a baby registry for you and Lydia."

"Get the hell out. Both of you."

"You seem a little stressed, bud. Perhaps if you'd

taken Peaches up on her offer last night you'd be able to focus better."

I rub my forehead with my hand before responding. "Has it ever occurred to you that her name isn't Peaches?"

"Jesus Christ, Rhys. Her name is Claire. I was taking comedic liberties, lighten up."

Claire. Meghan. Sara. Christine. Staci. Susan. Amy. Penny. Jessica. Etcetera.

Is there a girl from Double Diamonds I haven't fucked? Does remembering their names when I see them again instead of calling them 'sweets' make me less of an asshole? I'm starting to suspect that it doesn't. How is it that only weeks ago I'd have laughed at this entire conversation? Weeks ago I'd have fucked Peaches, given her a big tip and thought nothing of it.

Because weeks ago I hadn't kissed a girl in a bar.

A girl who looks at me with her innocent wide eyes and face full of hope. A girl who thinks I'd call, remember her birthday and what her favorite flavor of ice cream is, or that she prefers milk chocolate over dark. Things I wouldn't remember, things I never remember. A girl who has no idea what a dirty pervert I am, or how many women have come before her. How many relationships I've fucked up, how many women I've paid to make me feel good when I couldn't even be bothered to fake my way through dating a woman—or even taking one to dinner—long enough to get to the transaction of orgasms.

I tap open a new report on my laptop and try to focus.

"Do you ever worry that all we do is work and fuck?" I ask the question out loud, not really sure who I'm directing it at or expecting an answer.

They've been with me since the beginning of this journey. They were among the first people I brought on board after I located this property four years ago, a half-finished resort that had been abandoned when the previous investment group ran out of funding midway through construction.

We managed the initial phases of the project remotely, flying in and out of Vegas as the need arose. Just under a year ago we made the official move to Vegas, moving in to our executive suites on the thirty-fourth floor as the remainder of the hotel was still undergoing final construction. We've been living like perverted bachelors in a whorehouse ever since.

"Not really, no," Canon replies, tapping on his phone. "You coming with us to the club tonight?"

"Yeah, maybe," I say mostly so he'll stop asking. Maybe I will, I don't know. I can't think straight. The opening is so close. So goddamned close. Years of work about to come to fruition and it needs to be perfect. If this venture fails the damage it will do to the company would be colossal. My family's company. It's messing with my head. This hotel, this resort, it's my moment. Mine. My cousin Jennings has already taken over as CEO of the family company. My mother has been head of the North American division of the company since I was in junior high, with no signs of stepping aside.

Truth be told, I didn't want either of those jobs. I never did. I wanted something of my own. Something virgin and uncharted that I could build from the ground up. Or mid-construction-up, as it were. Something new, that would add to the company legacy, a project that would grow the family empire instead of simply contributing to it.

"Vince has something going on tonight in the back room," Canon cajoles. The back fucking room. Officially, it's the equivalent of a high-roller room. Pricey lap dances.

Unofficially, you're not paying for the lap dance. You're paying for the extras. Hand jobs, blow jobs, sex. You're paying to take the party off-site. An hour, a night, a weekend. Unofficially, of course.

How many times have I been to the back room? Asked for something more than a lap dance? Chosen from a selection of willing women as if I was selecting a value meal from a fast-food drive-thru?

I'm not good enough for her. I'd ruin her. Break her heart, crush that wide-eyed optimism that radiates from her, from the top of her head to the tips of her toes. I'd fuck her like a whore and forget to call because that's what I do. That's who I am.

She thinks I'm a good man. I can see it on her face when she thinks I'm not looking. I can see it on her face when she knows I am. When she rocked her warm pussy against my thigh. When she bit her lip and spread her hands across my chest. When she watches me make an espresso with the industrial coffee machine. I think she almost came last week when I put my own cup in the break room dishwasher.

Too easy. Too easy to impress, too easy to ruin.

Too fucking optimistic when what I like is the satisfied look on a woman's face after I've made her come, followed by the look of her ass walking out the door with a handful of cash tucked into her bag that guarantees me she understands what it was. That there was no miscommunication about my interest in her beyond getting off.

Besides which, even if I wanted something

different, I don't have the time. Two weeks until opening. Two. Weeks. My entire family will be in for the grand opening. My parents. My cousin Jennings and his new fiancée. My grandmother. My aunts and uncles and a smattering of cousins.

I want them to be proud of what my team and I have accomplished here in Vegas and no, it doesn't escape my attention that personally they have nothing to be proud of me for.

"How do you know what Vince has planned for tonight? Did you golf with him again today?"

"No. Got an email."

"You're on a mailing list for Double Diamonds?" I ask slowly, not sure this is real. "What the hell do they need to send emails for? To give customers a heads-up when they're running low on singles?"

"Everyone has a newsletter, Rhys. Don't be a dick. Besides, this is just for the back room customers, not for everyone."

"To notify us of what? Half-priced lap dances?"

"Auctions."

"Same thing."

"It's not an auction for reduced-price lap dances, Rhys. It's a virgin auction."

"Jesus Christ, Canon." I shake my head.

"No shit, really?" Lawson looks up from the game with interest and begins thumbing through his phone. "I didn't get that email," he mutters.

"It probably went to spam," Canon tells him this as if this is a normal conversation. "Check your junk mail. So you in?" Canon looks at me expectantly, unfazed by the concept, and I can't fault him. I can't say the idea doesn't make me a little hard.

"I told Brady I'd stop by tonight. I need to run some numbers with him about that idea we had for opening a satellite location of Hennigan's inside the Windsor."

"Lydia won't be at Brady's tonight," Canon tells me.

"How do you know that?" If he's doing one of his creepy security stalking things on her I'm going to be pissed. Sometimes he hacks people just because he can, or because he's bored. Or curious. Or because it's fucking Wednesday. Canon with time on his hands isn't good for anyone.

"Because she's going to be at Double Diamonds," he says, handing his phone to me.

His words hit me in slow motion. Logically I know I'm processing what he's saying in the blink of an eye, but illogically, it feels like it takes me a few minutes to get there.

Lydia.

Up for auction.

In the back room at Double Diamonds.

A virginity auction.

A goddamned virgin?

What did I say to her in the bar? What kind of filth did I whisper in her ear? I asked her how she liked to fuck, for Christ's sake. I told her I wanted her to choke on my cock. I talked to her like she was an experienced whore, not an innocent virgin.

Did she answer me? Or did she just smile and duck her head? Bite her lip and suggest we move to her apartment? I thought her a sweet little tease, too likely to want more from me. Like dinner or a repeat. Or worse, my time.

I wondered why my pants were still on and why she was rocking one out on my leg like it was her freshman year in high school. But a virgin? A twenty-two-year-old virgin, for fuck's sake. The thought never entered my mind.

Why in the hell is she doing this? Selling herself? She has a job and a place to live, so what in the hell is her end game? Money? Is it all about the money for her? What was I? A diversion? A practice run? A potential mark?

I thought she was different. Real. Too real for me was my worry, wasn't it? When it turns out she's just my type—for sale. The thought makes me itchy, worry about what else I've been wrong about clawing at me. My fingers inch into a fist, imagining her leaving that auction with any random entitled prick who can afford her. Someone who will whisper filth into her ear and fuck her like a whore.

Someone like me.

"How much?" I ask Canon, my jaw tight. I know I'm fucked up, because a good man would not be having the thoughts I'm having right now.

"It's an auction, not a buy now," he replies. "Bidding starts at a hundred grand."

FIFTEEN

LYDIA

"ARE YOU SERIOUSLY going to do this, Lydia? All fun aside, it's a little drastic. A lot drastic. You don't have to do this. Are you sure?"

I've never seen Payton nervous before and it does make me question just how far I've veered from the lane of sanity. Yet I'm sure. Sure that I'm going to do this. I'm reasonably sure that Vince will follow through and get Rhys here. Half-sure that Rhys will be interested. Semi-sure that Vince won't double-cross me and sell me into an underground sex ring, never to be seen or heard from again.

This is pretty dumb.

But I've got Payton, so it's not as if I'm here alone. And if we both disappear she's left instructions with her cousin about where to look for us. He's in law enforcement, which won't help us at all if we're dead.

Wow. This plan sounded so much better before I thought it through. I have a flutter of panic, and by flutter I mean a punch to the stomach. How exactly did I get here? This happened too fast. Yesterday Payton told me about Rhys and the hookers and this morning I concocted this insane plan and tonight I'm going up for auction.

Yet the thought of leaving, of running out of here, of going home, of opening that dating app Payton helped me set up and replying to any one of the men who've messaged me... it's not what I want. I want Rhys. And I need to know if he wants me too. Even if by the most unorthodox means ever concocted.

"The thing is, Payton, he just does it for me. I think he might be my swan." I fidget with the silk robe covering the lingerie I'm wearing. White. Staci insisted it be white. Once we'd come to terms Vince sent me to Staci for orientation. Orientation—his word, not mine. I wasn't sure if he was mocking me or not, but in any case Staci set me up with everything I needed.

We went to the mall, in case you're wondering. She said we didn't have time to do an online order, so she took me to Victoria's Secret. I told her there was no way I would be parading around in a thong in front of anyone. She'd blinked at me and then laughed, a little incredulously, before picking out a pleated babydoll with spaghetti straps and a lot of cleavage. She let me get matching lace panties that covered my butt though. The top half of my butt anyway. My cheeks are definitely hanging out, but at least it's not a thong.

"What the hell do swans have to do with anything?"

"They mate for life."

"But you haven't mated with him."

"I know," I say, dragging out the word, "but swans don't just randomly pick another swan and go at it, Payton. They choose carefully so they don't accidentally mate for life with just any random idiot swan that crosses their paths. They choose. Carefully."

"Wow."

"I know, right?"

"No, I meant wow, you're a nerd. Did you get a swan badge?"

"There's no swan badge," I retort with a roll of my eyes. "It was the 'animals in nature' badge," I mumble. "The point is I want it to be him. I want Rhys to devirginate me."

"I thought we agreed you weren't going to use that word anymore."

"I know, but it's a real word, Payton. A legitimate Merriam-Webster word, not an Urban Dictionary word."

There's a pause while Payton simply stares at me. "You realize we would not have been friends if we met in high school, right?"

"I wasn't that bad!" I protest. "I was sort of cool in high school."

"I'll have to take your word on that, tiger," Payton replies, but her expression does not indicate that she is taking my word on this. "Listen, we need to have a talk."

"What?" I eye Payton in the mirror. We're in the dressing room at Double Diamonds awaiting my big sale. I've got to say, this place has been nothing like I'd imagined it. The dressing room is really nice, much like Vince's office. It feels more like a spa locker room than a place of disrepute. Lockers, showers, a long mirrored counter for doing hair and makeup. There's a coffee station too, but just regular coffee. They don't have one of those fancy coffee machines like we have at the Windsor. I should tell Vince to add one, I think, then start to smile. As if I work here now and can make suggestions. Ha.

Payton turns me to her and takes my hands in

hers, waiting until I've given her my full attention. "You know what a penis looks like, right?"

"Payton! Oh, my word. I'm not totally clueless."

"And you know he'll want to put it inside of you, right?"

"Stop teasing me." I'm sure I'm beet red, a fact confirmed when I turn back to the mirror. "I know what sex is." I examine my reflection.

"Okay, just making sure. I would never send my girl into battle without a roadmap."

"It's game plan," I murmur. "You wouldn't send me into battle without a plan."

"Sure, whatever. I would never send you into battle without knowing what a penis looks like, is the point. Speaking of, do you have any questions?"

Err, no? "I don't think so?" Shoot, should I? Have questions? What questions would I have? I understand what sex is. I'm not uninformed, just inexperienced. I examine my nails, painted pale pink during my manicure this afternoon. Toes to match. I've been buffed and polished, hair blown out and makeup expertly applied. I'm wearing more makeup than I'd normally wear but I like it. I look like a more dramatic version of me. Add in the virginal lingerie and I'm feeling a bit like a bride on her wedding day.

But it's not my wedding day.

Definitely not.

"No, I don't have any questions, but maybe I'll text you later? If something comes up?"

"Okay. Feel free to ask me anything, or text me naked pictures of Rhys. Either-or. Just check in when you can."

"Will do. Check in, I mean. I'm not texting you naked pictures of Rhys."

"Okay, wow. I'm really starting to feel like I do all

the giving in this friendship, but tonight is your big night, so we can work on our friendship goals later."

"Deal."

"In case we don't get to talk later"—Payton pulls me into a hug, careful not to mess up my hair or makeup—"I just want you to know I'm proud of you, Lydia. As weird as it is to be proud of you for this, I am."

"Don't be proud yet. We don't even know if this worked. This might end with Vince selling me to a seedy businessman from Iowa. We don't really know yet, do we?"

A cough alerts me to the fact that we're not alone. I turn at the sound to find Vince has strolled in, hands in pockets and what I think is an amused expression on his face. Which is sorta impressive because from what I've learned about Vince he's not one to give any of his feelings away.

"Iowa's a very nice place. It's the ones from Maryland you want to watch out for."

Oh, crap. He heard that.

"Haha, you kidder, you." I'm trying for deflection because I'm not entirely sure how to handle Vince.

"I'm serious," he responds, his eyes flicking to Payton. "As a skydiver."

There's a pause as Payton eyes him, her brow furrowed while she considers him. Then she smiles. "Yeah, that was a good one. Skydiving safety is no joke."

Vince inclines his head before turning back to me.

"It worked," he says. "He's here."

It worked. It worked? It worked! I'm ready to bounce up and down on my stripper heels but... maybe he's not here for me? Maybe he's here for a random lap dance or some hot wings? They do have ten different flavors of wing sauce and I'm just one flavor.

"He's made a preemptive offer."

A preemptive offer? So... he offered? I'm leaving here with him? This worked? It really worked?

"The offer is for me?" I have to confirm. I need the words. I need the confirmation before I get too excited. I need one hundred percent assurance that the offer isn't for a combo meal before I make a fool out of myself.

"Yes, you."

I turn wide eyes to Payton and then squeal, bouncing on my toes. But carefully, because I'm more of a kitten heel than a stiletto heel kind of girl and it wouldn't do to break my ankle right now and end up in the emergency room instead of in bed. Having sex. With Rhys!

"You said yes, right? To whatever he offered? I told you the opening bid you suggested was stupid high." When Vince and I talked numbers this morning I suggested ten thousand and he laughed in my face. Then he'd suggested a hundred, which I thought was a little low until he clarified he meant a hundred thousand dollars, and then I giggled so hard I had to bend forward with a hand clamped over my mouth to contain myself.

It's not like I'm skilled, you know? Plus I did some research on the internet when I concocted this plan and the average cost for sex in Nevada is somewhere between a few hundred and a few thousand dollars. I know virgins are a silly novelty, but a hundred grand? Please.

"Did he offer ten thousand like I suggested?" I ask, refraining from rolling my eyes in Vince's face for being right. Just barely. If he didn't scare me a little I'd absolutely roll my eyes.

"He offered two and asked me to cancel the auction."

"Thousand, right? Two thousand dollars?" It's a little disappointing because I was really hoping for ten thousand, but the money was never the point. "So it's done, right? I don't have to go out there now?" I'm flooded in relief at the idea that I might get to skip the humiliation of parading around in this nightie. My fingers are already itching to slip back into the outfit I arrived in and a pair of shoes that don't require ballerina-level balancing abilities.

"Two hundred thousand, Lydia. And I told him another insulting offer like that was going to get him escorted out of my club."

I hear Vince, but it's taking me a moment to piece together what he's saying, my heart thumping in overtime as I glance nervously over at Payton. How much did he just say? And why did he refuse? What have I gotten myself into?

"Um, Vince." I swallow hard before continuing. "Why did you turn him down? We had a plan."

"Because I've got my own plan, Lydia, and two hundred doesn't cut it for me. Not even close."

Oh, God. I've made a deal with a pimp and it's working out exactly like one would imagine a deal with a pimp works out.

SIXTEEN

LYDIA

"TIME TO LOSE THE robe and take a walk."

Take a walk. I grasp the sash of the silk robe covering me and twist the material in my hands. He means the stage in the VIP room. Staci showed it to me earlier so I know where I'm going, know what to expect. The VIP room is private, obviously. Separated from the main floor via a set of stairs. The dressing room is on the second as well and connects to the VIP via a short hallway. Or a really long hallway depending on your mindset.

It's an intimate room. I picture it in my mind as I slip the robe off my shoulders and hand it to Payton. As I follow Vince down the back hallway while my pulse rings in my ears and my heels click on the laminate flooring.

There's a small stage in the VIP room and it's more runway-shaped than the ones downstairs. A bit closer to how I'd originally imagined the club, but on a much smaller scale. There's a curtain at the end of the runway where the dancers enter—or so I'm told. No one was using the room earlier today when Staci walked me through. She showed me where I'd enter, we walked the stage together, the lights up high and the room empty. It felt like previewing an event space, not a rehearsal for the biggest night of my life.

"He's definitely here?" I question as we stand behind the curtain, watching a dancer I met earlier on stage. I wonder if she's the opening act? I suppose she is. I'm not sure what I thought they'd be doing until it was my turn, but wasn't expecting to wait for someone else to come off stage. She's a really talented dancer, too. Strong. Flexible, obviously. She's setting the bar really high for me and I'm not sure I like it. Not that I'm dancing, but the flexible thing.

It's loud. The entire place is loud, decibels higher than it was when I was here earlier.

"He's here," Vince assures me. I can't see the customers from my vantage point behind the curtain. The seating is cast in shadows from where I'm standing. It's not a large room, not many seats. It reeked of exclusivity and privacy when I viewed it earlier. When I convinced myself this would be easy. I'd think of the stage as a runway and imagine myself a model rather than a hooker, I thought.

I'm thinking a little differently right now.

"Why do men need it to be so loud in order to get laid?" I ask. The noise from downstairs is making the floors shake and I wish I could adjust the volume as easily as I do on my iPod.

Vince shakes his head and laughs. "We'll turn it down during the auction. It'll be over quick."

Quick for him maybe.

The song ends, the dancer exiting the stage, brushing past us on her way past. The music changes, like a cue that I'm up, and I feel sick. It's lower and hypnotic and sexy and terrifying.

"He's on the left," Vince says. "Let's go." Then he's

pushing through the curtain, holding it open so I've got no choice but to follow. Follow or turn and run like hell.

I follow, because these are not running heels.

The lights blind me for a moment as my eyes adjust, even though it's certainly not what I'd call bright on the stage. There's a spotlight, I realize. I'm on display like something pretty in a store window. Vince is speaking but I couldn't tell you what he's saying. I'm too busy blinking and breathing and putting one foot in front of the other.

Focus on the goal, Lydia.

I glance to the left and—and I don't see Rhys. I see the head of the legal department at the Windsor, Lawson McCall. My steps falter and I reach out and grab the pole to steady myself. Next to him is Canon Reeves, head of security. And then Rhys. Why didn't it occur to me that he'd bring his friends? Why didn't I just think? These are men I'll have to see again. At work. My knees feel like they're going to buckle so I steady myself, gripping the pole so tightly my knuckles turn white.

Maybe Rhys isn't here because he wants me. Maybe he's here to fire me. I summon the courage to drag my eyes up and dart another glance in his direction.

He's looking right at me.

He doesn't look happy.

He looks mad. Really mad.

I'm so getting fired.

A voice from the right calls something out and I turn my head, reminded I'm not alone in this room with Vince, Rhys and his friends. There are other bidders. Oh, God. The sound I heard was someone making a bid, for me. The man is older. Older than my dads. Handsome, hair graying at the temples. A sharp suit.

Then Rhys is saying something and my attention snaps back to him. He's wearing a suit too, I notice on second glance, because he's standing now, taking the jacket off. I wonder if he dressed for the auction. For me.

The older man is still speaking again. He's calling out numbers, nonsensical numbers to my ears. Rhys barks, "Enough," and then he's stepped onto the stage next to me, wrapping his jacket around me and physically turning me around. His hand is firmly on my back, pushing until my feet move, until I'm off the stage, until the curtain has fallen into place behind us.

"Get dressed," is all Rhys gets out before the curtain rustles again, Vince and Canon a moment behind us. "Now," Rhys adds, his eyes flashing when I continue to simply stand there, staring.

The hallway to the dressing room is a lot shorter on the way back than it was on the way to the stage, but it may be because I near-run down the hallway, not even caring about the heels or my ankles now. I push open the door and then collapse against it when it closes again.

"Nice jacket." Payton is sitting sideways in a stuffed leather chair, legs hanging over one side, her blonde head over the other, dangling grapes over her head. She bites one off the bunch and raises her brows at me. "That was quick."

"Payton." I push myself off the door, still shaking a little. I kick the heels off and they drop to the floor one clunk at a time. "That was horrible."

"What happened?" She sits up, eyes wide.

"Lawson is out there. And Canon!"

"Oh." She leans back in her chair. "Well, yeah. They're friends, so that makes sense."

"Why didn't it occur to me that they might be here? I'm so embarrassed." I pull Rhys' jacket closer around me before remembering his instructions to get dressed, but the jacket smells like him and I'm loath to take it off.

"Did Rhys win you or what?"

"I don't know."

"How can you not know?"

"Because I don't know. One minute I was standing on stage under a spotlight and the next he was wrapping me in his jacket and telling me to get dressed."

"Sounds like you're leaving with Rhys."

"Maybe," I agree while slipping my jeans over my hips. "I am so messed up, Payton."

"Agreed. But tell me why you think you're messed up so we're on the same page."

I shoot her a dirty look before turning my back to remove the silk negligee and put on the fancy lace bra that matches the panties I had on underneath. I don't think I've ever owned matching underwear before. Like, matching matching. Normal matching is a white bra and underwear that has white polka dots or stripes or something. I pull a shirt over my head before turning back to Payton as I free my hair from the shirt collar.

"Because it turns me on. The idea of leaving here with him when he's paid for the right. Even though I hated being on that stage, I liked it when he dragged me off and told me to get dressed. But really, who the hell is he to tell me to get dressed, you know? I'm in charge of me. I can wear a nightie in public if I want to. I can have sex with whoever I want to, whenever I want to. I know I don't need to justify myself for wanting Rhys to take control, to boss me around, to lead. But am I contributing to some outdated patriarchal model about sex because I like it?"

"Whoa."

"I know, right?"

"No," she says with a big sigh. "I thought we were going to talk about the sheet pajamas."

The door opens and we both turn. It's Vince. Vince with an actual smile on his face.

"After a small bidding war I got him to five."

"Got who to five?"

"Rhys," Vince says, looking at me like I'm crazy. "Wasn't that the entire point, Lydia?"

I replay those words in my head as I sink into one of the leather chairs in the dressing room. The chairs were another touch I wasn't expecting, along with the fresh fruit tray Payton was eating from, but now is not the time to focus on either of those things. "Five hundred thousand dollars, Vince?"

"I could have easily gotten him to a million, but I consider him to be a sort of friend, so I let him off the hook at five." Vince shrugs, a smirk tugging at his lip, as if charmed by either the idea of friendship or the exchange of half a million dollars, I'm unsure which. "You've really got him by the balls, haven't you?"

"I don't have him by the anything!" I shriek. "If I had any idea how to have him I wouldn't be here right now talking to you!" I suck in a breath before continuing. "He knows I don't have any secret sex skills, right? You didn't oversell me, did you? What did you promise him? What bidding war? What does he think he's getting for five hundred thousand dollars?" My voice gets louder when I repeat the amount, because it's insane and now I'm panicked. "Does he think he's getting a party? Because I'm not doing his friends or anything weird like that. I'm not."

"I would," Payton pipes in. "You only live once, am I right?"

"I've got no idea what the guy is into," Vince says. "You're the one who wanted him so badly." He shrugs as if what Rhys is or isn't into is no big deal. "Lydia, relax. What kind of a monster do you take me for?"

There's a long awkward pause because I don't really have an answer for that, do I? I have no idea what kind of monster Vince is or is not.

He raises an eyebrow at my silence and shakes his head. "You want me to spell it out? Pussy. Ass. Mouth. I told him you're on the pill. As for the rest of it, you'll let him know if something is too much or if you're uncomfortable. I'm not a goddamned sex broker, for fuck's sake. I'm doing you a favor."

He's not wrong. Then he adds two words that throw me for a loop.

"One month."

A month? I chew on my bottom lip, lipstick be damned, and stare at Vince without speaking. I bounce my knees and fidget with the hem of my shirt while I think. A month? We never talked about a timeframe because I'd assumed hookering was done in hourly increments.

But apparently that's negotiable.

And logically, a month is a huge win for me.

"I thought it was just one night," I finally say, tilting my head back to look at Vince. "Where did a month come from?"

"You've got to give and take when you're negotiating, Lydia. We gave a month, we got half a million."

That stupid half a million. It's ridiculous and makes me a little sick to my stomach. Maybe averaged out it isn't so bad? I do some quick math and determine it comes out to fifteen or sixteen thousand per night. Which is still too much, way too much. I hope Rhys isn't always this financially irresponsible. Then again I'm still using my parents' Netflix account so I shouldn't be so judgey.

"Are we actually talking about this? Is this conversation really happening?" Payton glances between Vince and I with a look of disbelief on her face. "She accepts," Payton tells him and then turns to me. "You accept. It's time to earn your Rhys badge."

SEVENTEEN

LYDIA

RHYS IS OUTSIDE WAITING for me. Outside as in he's pulling his car up to the back entrance.

I'm not sure if I should be offended by this use of the back entrance or if that's how he picks up all his girls.

Vince and Payton walk me to the door, Vince pushing it open and holding the door wide for me to pass through. "Have fun," he says, while Payton adds, "Break a dick!" as I step outside.

There's a car straight ahead, sporty and low, the engine purring and the headlights casting a wide beam across the parking lot. The passenger door is on my side so I don't have far to walk, for which I'm grateful, because even with flat shoes my knees are feeling a bit wobbly.

It's chilly, which for Vegas means it's dropped below sixty. The only coat I have with me is Rhys's jacket, folded over my arm. I hope he doesn't want to go anywhere, because I don't have a jacket of my own. It's already late though, and I can't imagine he has a walk in the park in mind for tonight. I hope he doesn't have a walk in the park on his mind for tonight. When I get to the car I open the passenger door and bend, peeking inside to make sure it's Rhys before I get in. Can you imagine if I hopped in the wrong car after all of this?

It's Rhys.

I slide in, pulling the door shut behind me. He's staring straight ahead and the car is in motion before I even have a chance to buckle up. I drop my bag on the floorboards, his jacket crushed in my lap, and grab the seat belt, clicking it into place as he accelerates out of the parking lot and merges into traffic.

He still hasn't looked at me.

"Hi," I offer, because I'm not sure what else to say and he's being weird.

He grunts in response.

I straighten his jacket again, smoothing it carefully so it doesn't wrinkle. Then I toy with the hem of my shirt, bunching the fabric nervously in my fingers because I don't care about wrinkles on my own clothing. When I shiver Rhys punches a button on the dash and warm air blows lightly from the vents.

"What were you thinking, Lydia?"

Okay, so we're talking now.

"What the hell were you thinking?"

And he's mad. Real mad.

"Is it the money?" I ask. "Because—" I don't get very far because he cuts me off.

"No, it's not the money, Lydia. Half a million wouldn't even cover the swag for the casino opening. You cost less than the party favors, so don't worry yourself about the money."

Wow.

He's rolled his shirt sleeves up to the elbow and his forearm muscles flex as he handles the wheel.

His jaw clenches and he's still not looking at me.

"Just tell me, was this always your plan?"

What? "No, of course not." This plan is less than two days old, so no. It's hardly even a plan, more of an irrational crazy idea.

"A goddamned virgin. I thought you were different, but fuck, Lydia."

"Wait, you're mad at me for something I haven't done? That's not even fair. It's discriminatory. You can't discriminate against me for being inexperienced."

"You let me whisper filth in your ear thinking you knew what the fuck I was talking about."

"I liked the filth!"

"Jesus Christ." He takes a hand off the wheel and drags it across his jaw as if he's stressed.

"Okay." My voice catches and I steady myself so I don't cry. "You're mad. I'm sorry. I just thought—" I stop myself from saying more. "Just take me back. You're obviously not interested in me. I don't know why you bid on me. Just take me back." Vince is going to kill me. Maybe literally, I don't know. He'll have to refund Rhys and he'll probably make me reimburse him for the money he lost which I'll never, not ever, be able to do. He'll charge interest and the balance will just keep getting bigger and bigger—as it does when you owe the mafia money—until I'm forced to make a deal that involves me burying a body or lying to the feds.

I literally cannot believe the effort I've gone through for this jerk.

"Take you back?" He laughs, but I don't particularly care for his tone. "I've paid in full. I'm keeping you."

"Whatever! Fine, if you want to."

"If I want to?" He exhales like I've exhausted him in the few short minutes we've been in the car together. "I don't have time for this right now, Lydia. In case you haven't noticed, I've got a lot on my plate right now."

"I know, but I looked it up on the internet and read that on average most couples have sex for seven to thirteen minutes and I don't mind if it's closer to seven minutes. We can be quick."

We're at a stoplight and he finally turns to look at me. "What?" His eyes flash in the dark, questioning, the tiny lines at the corners creasing as he tilts his head a fraction in my direction.

"You said you were pressed for time," I say slowly, not sure what he's not getting. "But it'll only take seven minutes." He doesn't say anything so I keep talking, wondering if I misunderstood what I read. "Maybe you could skip seven minutes of sleep tonight and you'd still be right on schedule." I think that sounds like a very reasonable resolution but he bends over the steering wheel and laughs so hard I'm afraid he's going to miss the light. "Or we can wait till after the opening," I offer and shrug, trying to pretend I'm not disappointed, like it's no big deal. But it's a very big deal. I am never losing my virginity. Like ever.

"This might be the best half mil I ever spent," he mutters but I'm not sure he's speaking to me. "What are you going to do with it anyway? The money?" The fingers of his right hand tap rapidly on the steering wheel as if he's agitated. I'm not sure if it's with me or the red light.

"Student loans," I reply, crossing my arms as I lie. I don't feel like talking to him about the money. I never wanted it, I only wanted Rhys. I only wanted more time with him. An opportunity to understand him a little better, to explore the connection I felt with him at the bar, the connection I know he felt as well. Maybe he wasn't as enamored with me as I was with him, but I know he felt something.

Besides, my plans for the money were small. My deal with Vince was for fifty percent. I was thinking fifty percent of ten thousand, not fifty percent of five hundred thousand. My plans will require some re-working.

"You know how it is. Those interest rates are no joke," I add, looking out the window to avoid looking at him.

"Okay," he says, but his tone indicates I'm full of it. That he doesn't believe me. That I'm a conniving money-grabbing hoe-bag.

We've arrived at the Windsor and Rhys guides the car into the employee parking section of the garage, but to a section I've not been to before. We access it though a lift gate marked 'private' and he slides into a numbered space and kills the engine. We sit in silence for a few seconds, Rhys staring straight ahead at the cinderblock wall, me side-eyeing him from the passenger seat.

"Okay, well." I un-click my seatbelt and open my door. Rhys follows suit and we meet at the trunk of the car, toe to toe. I glance up at him under my lashes but he's already turning, walking towards the elevators.

He punches a series of numbers into a keypad and the elevator doors open. We step on and I notice this elevator only stops at a handful of floors. The parking garage, floors two through four and thirty-four, where the executive suites are. I'm not even sure where this elevator lets out on four. Clearly it's private and meant as a personal elevator for the executive staff.

The doors open on thirty-four and it looks pretty much like the rest of the guest floors I've seen. Rhys leads the way, his footsteps near-silent on the plush carpet, before coming to a stop at a set of double doors. And then we're inside, standing in a large marbled foyer. Straight across, past a seating area with a large sectional sofa, are floor-to-ceiling windows with a view of the Strip. It's nice. It's also a little sad. It looks like a combination of a model home and a hotel suite. It doesn't look very lived-in.

"How long have you lived here?" I ask.

"A little under a year."

"Where's your stuff?"

"What stuff?"

"Books? A knickknack? Something that belongs to you?"

"It all belongs to me. I own the hotel."

That's one way of looking at it, I suppose.

"Thank you for the jacket," I offer, holding it out for him to take from me. His eyes drop down to the material in my hands as if he hadn't realized I was carrying anything. He takes it from me, along with my bag, and turns, disappearing down a hallway that I assume leads to his bedroom.

I continue to stand in the same spot because I've never sold my virginity before so I'm not sure what the proper protocol is, or what I'm supposed to do.

Rhys reappears and walks past me without a glance, heading to a bar situated at the far side of the living area. I follow slowly behind, staying on the opposite side of the bar as he pours himself a drink. A shot of something, I'm really not sure what. I'm not that familiar with alcohol either, truth be told.

I'm only twenty-two and I didn't do much underage drinking. By much I mean any.

"Can I have one?"

"Do you need one?"

His reply is curt, his eyes on mine as he knocks back his drink.

"Why are you being so mean?"

"Mean?" His brows rise in surprise. "Mean?" he repeats with a laugh. "I just saved you from creepy Stan and I'm mean?" He shakes his head. "Now you're stuck with creepy Rhys instead," he mutters to himself.

"I don't think you're creepy," I say, shaking my head in refusal. I didn't think Stan was creepy either, assuming he's referring to the older guy who was bidding on me, but I don't think it would be appropriate to mention that at the moment. He was super old and I didn't want to have sex with him, but he looked nice enough.

"I just bought you, Lydia. For sex."

"You buy lots of girls for sex," I answer because I'm not sure why it's such a big deal that he paid for me. It's not as if he hasn't done this before, but his eyes narrow and he seems annoyed again. "It wasn't against my will," I add, in case that wasn't clear to him. "It was my idea. The auction was my idea. I don't owe the mob any money. Not yet, anyway."

He sets a second glass on the countertop and fills both, sliding one over to me when he's done. I pick it up and hold the glass to my lips and even though there's not much in the glass I take a sip instead of knocking it back like he did.

"That's terrible," I sputter, setting the glass down.

"That's Scotch," he replies. "Do you always want things that you end up not liking, Lydia?"

135

"Not usually, no. But one time I bought an ugly sheet at Goodwill thinking it'd be cute when I turned it into pajama pants, but I was wrong." I hold my hands up in a gesture of defeat. "The pants were just as ugly as the sheet had been. I'm not sure that constitutes something I wanted though. It was more of a bad purchase situation but I got them at fifty percent off because they were marked with a pink tag and it was pink tag week so it was closer to an experiment than a bad purchase," I finish in a rush. I think I'm nervous. I wonder if I should try another sip of that awful Scotch? While I'm contemplating that something else occurs to me. "Maybe I'm a bad purchase? Why am I even here? I thought you were too busy to have sex? I could have just gotten a ride home with my roommate."

Rhys has rounded the bar while I babbled and now he's stopped directly in front of me. He places a finger under my chin and tilts my head up, placing a soft kiss on my lips.

"Why are you doing this to me?" he whispers in my ear, He doesn't seem so mad anymore.

"Is it happening right now? Are we doing the sex?"

"We're most definitely doing the sex," he confirms and takes my hand in his.

EIGHTEEN

LYDIA

"THIS IS WHAT YOU want?"

"Yes." I nod quickly and repeatedly. "Yes, yes, yes."

We've moved to his bedroom, another set of floor-to-ceiling windows, another priceless view of the Strip. A king-sized bed neatly made with the sheets turned down for the evening. I wonder if he has maid service or if he makes his own bed every day.

He kisses me again, a soft press of his lips against mine, and then he's moving about the room while I remain rooted to the spot, just inside the doorway. He unfastens his watch, sliding it from his wrist and placing it inside the top drawer of the dresser. His wallet follows and then he's unrolling his shirt sleeves.

"Fear isn't really my kink, Lydia."

I'm not afraid, just unsure. Unsure what to do with myself. Unsure what he wants. Unsure if I'm supposed to strip completely naked and lie down on the bed, or just strip down to my new bra and panties so he can take those off me himself.

"I'm not afraid, I just don't know what I'm supposed to do. And being in charge isn't my kink,

Rhys."

"So you want me to tell you what to do?"

"Would you?" I exhale in relief. Finally he's
getting it. "Boss me. Teach me. Talk dirty to me. I
like all of that. I'm good with instructions. And rules.
I love rules. They're so clear and unambiguous and
sexy."

He moves to stand in front of me, standing close
enough that I have to tilt my head back to look at
him.

"We can't be anything more than this, Lydia. One
month. I'm not looking for anything more than that.
This won't be some kind of happily-ever-after
fantasy." He strokes his hand down my arm and I
shiver in response. His eyes are steady on mine,
ensuring I'm listening. "Just sex. That's the rule."

"Relax, Rhys. I'm not going to fall in love with you
just because you're my first." I don't think. Maybe.
There's likely only a solid fifteen percent chance of
that happening. At best.

"Your first." He repeats those words slowly, his
breath warm against my temple. "I'll ruin you for
anyone else." He says it softly and I'm not sure if it's
a promise or a warning.

He walks me backwards to his bed, his hands on
my hips guiding me, his lips on mine, on my jaw,
trailing down my neck. My shirt is lifted. I raise my
arms and it's tugged over my head as the backs of my
thighs hit the mattress. He unbuttons my jeans and
lowers the zipper and I suppose I am a little bit
scared. But the exhilarated kind, like that feeling you
get when a rollercoaster makes the click-click-click
ascent to the top and you can't see where the dropoff
is but you know it's close, you know at any moment
you'll reach the apex and time will hold still for one

second, one second that feels like ten, and then you'll fly and flip and soar at speeds so fast all you can do is grip the safety harness with your hands and enjoy the ride, even though it's terrifying and you're not entirely certain you won't die.

Kinda like that.

He tugs my jeans over my hips and drags them down my legs, bending to free them from my ankles. I rest a hand on his shoulder and step out, one foot at a time.

"Sit," he tells me and I do. He's kneeled on the floor at the foot of the bed, my knees spread open to allow him between.

"This is nice," he says, drawing a fingertip along the swell of my breast where my new lace bra lies against my skin.

"Thank you," I say, my eyes on his fingertip as it skims across one breast and then dips into my cleavage and up, repeating the trip across the other. "The panties match," I add in case he missed it and because it's sort of a big deal.

"That they do," he murmurs in agreement and then kisses the spot under my right ear. His breath whispers across my neck while his facial hair lightly scratches and the combination makes me all sorts of crazy. "Let's take a look, shall we?" He gives me a gentle push back so I'm resting on my elbows, while running a finger down the center of my stomach until he reaches his destination. "Very nice."

He's not wrong. They are very nice.

Then he bends his head and kisses me. Right there. Right over the fancy lacy panties and I think I might die. Because it's embarrassing. Because it feels good. Because I want him to do it again and again and again. Rhys presses his nose into my panties and inhales, his eyes on mine, and ohmygod do men do that? Rhys does that. I bet Rhys does lots of things and he's going to do them to me. I bite my lip as Rhys hooks his thumbs into the sides of the material and tugs them down my thighs. His fingers skim the sensitive spots under my knees and down my calves until the material clears my ankles.

"You're bare," he says, rubbing his thumb across the empty patch of skin on my pubic bone. "You weren't before."

"You saw the outfit I was wearing. I thought it was best if I took it all off, because of the lighting and stuff. On stage."

His jaw ticks.

"Did you shave it or get it waxed?"

"I shaved it," I respond and I'm not sure why it's so hard to eke out so few words but I'm kinda breathless, my heart beating so quickly.

"Next time you'll let me do it," he says, his thumb continuing its examination.

"Why? Did I miss a spot?" I try to close my thighs, but he's between them and his shoulders are very wide so the movement doesn't gain me much closure.

"No." He uses his other thumb and spreads me open and licks me and oh, holy hell. My head drops back with a groan and I tighten my thighs on his shoulders.

"Then why do you want to do it?"

"Because it will turn me on. Spreading your sweet legs apart. Lathering you with shaving cream. Running a razor carefully along every inch of your pussy while you blush from head to toe."

He licks me again, a slow sweep with his tongue from bottom to top, ending with sucking my clit between his lips. I grip the bed cover in my fists and try not to grind my pelvis into his face. Holy—I've not, I don't know what this is supposed to feel like but ohmygod. His tongue is so freaking warm and soft and then the scruff on his chin follows and it's lightly abrasive and the mix of sensations is doing all sorts of things to me.

"I'll take my time doing it too," he continues, this time nuzzling his nose into my inner thigh and kissing his way back to my core. "I'll linger. I'll examine every inch of you. I'll make it so you'll never be able to shave yourself again without being turned on remembering how it felt when I did it for you."

I can't answer him because I'm breathing too hard. I like this idea very much.

"My good girl has a very wet pussy, doesn't she? You want me to play with it? Get my fingers wet?"

Yes. Oh, God, yes.

He rims the tip of his finger around my entrance, around and around, and then he flicks my clit with it and I'm on the edge. And then he does it again, and again. When he finally slides a finger inside of me I'm more than wet enough but the intrusion is still foreign to me and I tense. I tense all over, my thighs and my knees and my fists bunched into the comforter, but most especially where his finger is. But he doesn't stop, he sucks on my clit until I relax, then he does something magic with his finger until I come. I can feel myself fluttering around that finger, and oh, holy cow, an orgasm feels different with penetration and I want more. I want *him*. The moment he withdraws that finger I want it back, I want more than a finger. I feel empty and achy and I need him inside of me soon or I'll combust.

He pulls me to my feet and he kisses me and he

tastes like me and it's dirty and shocking and sorta oddly thrilling and primal. He unsnaps my bra. The straps slip down my arms until it falls to the floor and then I'm naked. I'm naked with Rhys. This is the best day of my life. Except he's not naked.

"You're still dressed. Am I supposed to"—I gesture to his shirt—"am I supposed to or are you supposed to? Or do you like to keep your clothes on when you have sex?"

He laughs, his eyes dancing in amusement as he unbuttons his shirt and shrugs it off. "No, I'm not going to fuck you with my clothes on, Lydia."

"Oh, thank goodness. I've really been wanting to see you naked. For a long time. Like weeks. Since the bar. The first time at the bar, not the second time. Can I take off your pants?" My fingers hover at his waistband, poised to unbutton and unzip but needing the nudge of permission.

"Please," he says and then my fingers are in motion, unbuckling, unbuttoning, unzipping. It's harder to do this in reverse, removing someone else's pants instead of your own, but I manage. I'd manage even if it was a thousand-piece puzzle instead of just a zipper and a button because I want his pants off pretty badly.

When I've got the pants undone they drop to the floor and then the only thing separating me from sex is a pair of briefs, so I make short work of those.

He's beautiful. Head to toe. I could spend all night looking at him, all month, forever. But I don't have forever or even all night since Rhys is worried about his schedule so I take in as much as I can as fast as I can.

Because oh, holy crap, I know what Rhys Dalton looks like naked. The smattering of hair across his chest. His toned abs and flat stomach and the trail of hair from his belly button to his cock. The birthmark on his left hip and the definition of the lines that form on his abs. I send a silent prayer to baby Jesus that I'll get a good look at his butt before this is over because I need to know exactly what it looks like under those suit pants. Then too soon, he's moving me onto the bed because this is it. This is the sex.

Except it's not.

NINETEEN

NOT YET, BECAUSE HE spends forever—way longer than seven minutes—just kissing me. Kissing and caressing. My neck, my breasts, my hips, my thighs. Long calming strokes of his hands, gentle brushes of his fingertips until he's worked his way down my body and he's resting between my legs again. And then he's doing the tongue and finger thing all over again and I'm so, so wet and slick but when he adds a second finger it feels so freaking tight and I've seen firsthand that he's a lot bigger than two fingers so I'm not sure how this is going to work.

"You're really good at tongues," I manage to say after I've come a second time and he's kissing the insides of my thighs like they're interesting.

"Has anyone ever gone down on you before, Lydia?"

"No. Is that okay? Am I doing it wrong?" Am I coming too fast? Too slow? Too loud? Too quiet? Worry claws at me as I wonder if other girls are better at coming than I am, which is dumb. I know it's dumb but I've got nothing to compare this to. Maybe he went down on me twice because he wanted a different reaction? I don't freaking know.

Then I feel him smile against my thigh, which is a weird yet lovely sensation. "You're perfect," he says, placing another kiss on my thigh, his bottom lip dragging against my skin, the tickle of his facial hair affecting me in bizarre places.

He places a kiss on my stomach, directly below my belly button, and tells me again that I'm perfect and I believe him. It helps that I can feel his cock brushing against my leg when he does so, and it's hard. He's hard everywhere really. His body is so firm and taut and warm and perfectly heavy on top of mine, like a weighted blanket of male. He works his way back up my body, kissing and petting and making my body strum with more anticipation than an entire amusement park of rollercoasters ever could. Then he kisses me again, our legs entwined and his cock lying heavily on my stomach. I want to touch him. I should touch him, right? Like touch touch?

"Tell me what to do," I plead, rubbing my hands up and down his forearms.

"Do anything you want," he says, pressing another soft kiss to my lips. He's lying so close to me, I can see the tiny lines around his eyes and the pulse beating in his neck. I run a fingertip along his eyebrow just because I can, because he's here in bed, with me. And then I snake my hand between us and run my fingertips along the length of him. His eyelids flutter closed and his jaw clenches, a small hiss of breath escaping when I touch him, so I feel emboldened to do more. To wrap my finger and thumb around him—as much as I can—and drag my hand from root to tip. He feels impossibly long and thick and I'm anxious about fitting him inside of me, but aching for it at the same time. I feel wet and needy and desperate and eager. And nervous—that too.

"Am I doing this okay?" I've wrapped my hand around the length of him and am slowly but firmly stroking him. I'm fascinated with the head, the slight ridge of skin letting me know I've reached the tip, the way the skin feels a bit smoother here. The tiny slit at the top, the bit of slick pre-cum that I found and rubbed between my finger and thumb before using it to massage the head.

"Perfectly," he says on another hiss of a breath. I glance at him from under my lashes and then lean forward and place a kiss on his chest.

"Should I use my mouth too?"

"Fuck, no," he says and his cock jerks in my hand.

Oh. My hand pauses, unsure, until he covers mine with his own and increases the pressure, continues the rotation of strokes up and down. Squeezing harder, moving faster, twisting our wrists together.

"Not now. Anytime but right now."

"Okay." I smile at him and try to rub myself on his thigh because I don't really want his cock in my mouth right now either. I want him to move this to the next step.

This time he does.

He spreads my thighs and kneels between them, placing a pillow under my hips.

Oh, God, this is happening. My chest rises and falls with my breathing as Rhys positions me, hooking my spread thighs over his arms, pinning me wide open. He rubs his palms down the insides of my thighs then positions himself at my entrance. I can feel the head of his cock at my folds, I can see everything too, with the way he's arranged us. I scrunch my eyes shut and hold my breath as he makes a noise, a combination of a laugh and an exhale.

"Relax, Lydia."

"Yeah, okay." I exhale and open my eyes. I wiggle my hips on the pillow. I'm relaxed.

He taps the head of his cock against me, like a slap. I like that. I clench and he must like that because he groans, his eyes on the spot where he's attempting to join us. He smooths his hands across my thighs again, the gesture comforting. Then he circles my clit with his thumb and it feels so good. It feels wonderful, until he notches the head of his cock inside of me and I tense again, breath held.

"Relax, Lydia," Rhys repeats himself, his jaw clenched, the muscles in his neck tense.

The thing is, I really want this, I do. But also I never purposely hurt myself and I don't see any way around this hurting. He slides the head of his cock in and then out again and I'm so slick and wet and ready that it doesn't hurt, it feels like I want more, but when he pushes farther I tense. My shoulders, my legs, my everything.

I am the worst hooker in the history of hookering.

"I'm—"

Sorry, is what I'm about to say but I don't get that far because Rhys pinches the inside of my thigh, hard. And when he does that it's like all of my nerve endings focus on that one spot and I can't focus on tensing anywhere else so I don't, I relax and focus on that bite of pain on my thigh and in that moment of distraction he thrusts into me with one rough jab of his hips and he's in, he's in, and holy fuck that hurts. Distraction or not, that hurts. Like a tear, like I'm being split in half and it burns and he's so deep and he's tensed over me, not moving, breathing hard, holding himself still, waiting on me to do something, I think, but I'm not sure what or how I feel and I think I might cry so I cover my face with my hands.

He lets go of my legs, leaning over me and bracing himself on his forearms next to my head, the movement altering the angle of my hips and the way he feels inside of me and—oh, God—is that better or worse? I'm not sure. He moves my hands and kisses my temple.

"Are you okay?"

"I don't know." Maybe?

"Am I hurting you?"

"Yes!" Duh.

"Fuck." He starts to move, immediately lifting off of me, easing out of me.

"No!" I sling my arm around his neck and pull him back to me. "Don't go. It's a normal hurt. I think. I have no idea."

His lips twitch into a smile, though there's tension near his eyes as if it's paining him to go this slow, to hold this still.

"Tell me what it feels like."

"What this feels like, right now?"

"Yes. Please," he adds and it's both a demand and a plea. He kisses my jaw and the movement causes another slight adjustment to positioning, another tiny new sensation to adjust to.

"What it feels like to have you inside of me?" I flush saying it. I can feel the color cover my cheeks as the words leave my mouth.

"Yes, exactly that. Tell me."

"Like you're breaking me, but also like I might like it."

He looks fascinated by my responses. His eyes

flickering across my face. His gaze intent.

"Full. It feels really full. It feels hot and tight and pinchy. Is pinchy a word? It feels like stretching after a long run, and achy. But it also feels good. The full feeling is really nice, like I have no idea how I ever lived without feeling it." I move my hands to his hips and run them along his skin, my fingers gripping his ass while I wiggle beneath him, adjusting to the penetration and realizing the pain has subsided into a dull ache, but also into a needy ache. Like I might want something more.

"What else?" he prompts. He kisses the corner of my mouth, a soft brush of his lips, and I don't know why that makes me hot but it does.

"It feels like pressure. Like all this pressure is there building or pulsating. Can I say pulsating? And like I might want you to move?" It's a question-slash-statement because I'm not entirely sure. "Not off of me!" I add, gripping his hips tighter in my hands, afraid I've just given bad directions. "Not off of me. In me." I buck my hips as much as I can from my position beneath him.

Rhys holds my head in his hands and kisses me—a long, wet kiss filled with tongues and nips along my bottom lip—and then he eases off, back to his knees, still buried inside of me as he repositions my spread thighs over his, his forearms under my knees supporting me and keeping me wide open.

I can see where we're joined at this angle. My pelvis is raised off the bed, my hands back to gripping the comforter in clenched fists. He pulls out of me and I feel the loss immediately. The slow slide of his body leaving mine, the feeling of fullness easing into emptiness. He pauses with just the head of his cock inside of me and we can both see the blood. His dick is wet, covered in me and streaks of red, and I suck in a breath because it's a little weird, a little base, a little primal and my feelings about all of this are raw, but Rhys doesn't look freaked out in the least. He looks like he's super into it so I exhale and try to relax.

Then he flexes his hips and drives back into me and I don't really care what his dick is covered in as long as he doesn't stop doing that. He repeats the motion, a long slow drag out followed by a smooth deep glide in, and I decide that I like sex very much.

"That's a good girl," he praises me when I lift my hips to meet his and I like hearing that almost as much as I like sex. Positive reinforcement is totally my thing and being called a good girl while his dick is inside of me is a filthy twisted spin on positive reinforcement that I find suits me just fine.

"I'm glad it's you," I say softly. "I'm glad I'm doing this with you."

His eyes shut for a moment and he swallows. A drop of sweat runs down his chest and I give an experimental clench around his cock where it's buried deep inside me and everything gets impossibly tighter and that feeling of pressure and heat gets more intense.

"That's good," he groans, his eyes opening, gaze hooded. Then he leans over me again, bracing himself on one hand and using the other to bend my knee towards my chest. That feels different, but I don't have time to think or adjust too much because he's pounding into me now. Fast. Quick and deep. Hard. My tits bounce from the thrusts and the sound of his skin slapping against me echoes throughout the room. The lights from the Strip flash and sparkle and glow just beyond the windows and I feel like I'm close to doing all of those things as well. So close.

Rhys bends my leg farther so my knee is practically at my ear and ohmygod he's even deeper and harder and bigger this way and then his thumb is back on my clit and yes, firm yes, I like sex. I arch my back and dig my fingertips into Rhys's forearms and he's whispering the good girl thing again in my ear and all the pressure and friction ignite and my legs are tensing and I'm coming and it's all so tight and warm and I squeeze my eyes shut and a stream of 'ohs' fall from my mouth.

Rhys groans when I tighten around him, holding himself still over me, and then he's moving again, making short jabs with his hips until he's coming too, the tension leaving his jaw and he's beautiful, so beautiful, and I can't believe I got to do this with him.

"That felt like a wave," I tell him, when he's done, collapsed on top of me, breathing hard. "Like a warm intense wave, or maybe the best part of a rollercoaster or like flying." I run my fingers along his back, exploring the lines with my fingertips, running my nails lightly across his skin. "It felt different with you inside of me, the orgasm. Different than it felt with your thumb or your mouth. And wet. It felt wetter. Feels wetter. I think it's probably because you just came in me. It feels kinda messy, but like a mess from a good party you don't want to clean up yet." He's silent, save for the sound of his breathing. "Sorry, I'm not any good at dirty talk."

"Are you trying to kill me?" He pants the question into my ear.

"No." I shake my head against the pillow under my head. "Of course not. I want to do that again."

He eases out of me and I feel an instant void from the loss. And sore, I feel sore and exposed and vulnerable. Rhys gets off the bed and walks through an open door, flipping on a light as he enters the bathroom. His ass is perfect, just like I thought it would be. Tight and muscular and there's a little dimple thing I need to explore next time.

I sit up on the bed, not sure what I'm supposed to do now. Should I leave? That's what he paid me for, right? So I'd get out when he was done? Am I allowed to use the bathroom first? His normal girls probably just get the hell out, right? I spot my bag sitting on a chair across the room so I get up, wincing as I do. Yeah, I'm gonna feel that tomorrow. I'm slipping a t-shirt from my bag when Rhys returns.

"What are you doing?"

"I thought this was the part where you slapped me on the ass and told me it was time to go, sweetness."

"Sit down," he says, nodding to the bed. He doesn't look amused by my assessment of how tonight ends so I drop my shirt and return to the bed. Which is when I realize I just lost my virginity on a fluffy white duvet cover and there's no coming back from that for the fluffy white duvet cover and I am mortified. Five hundred thousand dollars and I ruined his bedding. I'm a terrible, terrible hooker.

I start to pull the duvet from the bed when he stops me.

"What are you doing?" he asks again, resting a hand on my arm. He looks confused and I wonder if I'm behaving rationally.

"I ruined your bed."

"Lydia, who cares?"

I do. This entire apartment is pristine and perfect

and I'm like a messy rescue puppy.

"I'll call housekeeping and have a new one sent up," he says softly, running his hand down my arm. "Go take a shower."

"When you say you'll call housekeeping you mean you'll meet them at the door and then you'll get rid of this bedding, not hand it to someone I'll bump into in the employee cafeteria on Monday, right?"

"I'll take care of it."

"Okay." I nod to myself a couple of times and then Rhys is gently pushing me in the direction of the bathroom so I go. I take an obscenely long shower and I think about my feelings while I use his shampoo and body wash because that's all that he keeps in his shower.

By the time I return Rhys is sitting in bed, back to the headboard with a laptop propped on his lap. The entire apartment is dark save for a bedside lamp and the glow coming from his laptop. The Strip view has been blocked with some kind of blackout blind system. The bedding has been replaced and straightened and fluffed and I wonder again if he makes his own bed normally or if housekeeping comes every day.

I'm wrapped in a towel because I didn't think to bring anything into the bathroom with me. My hair is still damp and I'm holding onto the edges of the towel way harder than necessary since Rhys has already seen me naked.

He's wearing cotton pajama pants, his legs stretched before him and his chest bare. He doesn't look as if he plans on driving me home, but that's not really his job, is it?

"Should I call an Uber?" I ask, inching towards my bag.

"What?" He looks up from his laptop, a look of confusion on his face.

"An Uber," I repeat. "Or a cab?"

"You can stay," he says, nodding at the bed beside him.

Okay.

"What should I wear?" I ask, opening my bag and taking out the white negligee I wore on stage earlier. "Do you want me to wear this?" I notice my clothing has been picked up from the floor, folded and draped over the chair with my bag.

"No," he replies. "Not that." I think I'm annoying him now. "What do you normally wear to bed?"

Sheet pajamas, I think to myself. Nothing he'd want to see. "I didn't bring anything I'd normally wear to bed," is what I tell him, the negligee still dangling from my hand. His eyes flicker over it and then drop back to his laptop.

"Take a shirt from the middle drawer," he says, already typing again.

The middle drawer, I find, is soft t-shirt nirvana. I select a blue one and slip back into the bathroom to change in some misguided need for privacy.

'll be nodding off in a matter of minutes, which is lame because I'm in Rhys' bed and I should be soaking up the experience. But I did do an awful lot today and Rhys is working so I don't think he wants to cuddle or anything.

I'm about to nod off to the oddly lulling sounds of Rhys typing on his laptop when I remember something. "Sorry that took like ten times longer than seven minutes," I tell him, and then I'm out.

TWENTY

RHYS

I WAKE UP WITH a raging hard-on and Lydia's ass pressed against my cock. Because I'm on my side with my arm wrapped around her middle. Because we're spooning. We're goddamned spooning. Fuck. I roll onto my back, disgusted with myself.

For so many reasons.

God, the look on her face when she saw the duvet last night, like I'd give a fuck about the bedding? Fucking virgins.

I've never fucked a virgin before. I've never been anyone's first and I'm wondering if this was a mistake. A giant goddamned mistake. I rub my hands over my face and stare at the ceiling. She's the only perfect thing in this apartment and she's worried about ruining my bedding? Fuck the bedding. The only thing getting ruined in this apartment is her because I'm a depraved asshole who bought a virgin.

Remembering her blood on my dick is making me uncomfortably hard. The sweet blush on her cheeks, Jesus. Is that supposed to turn me on? Because it does. Taking her innocence. Knowing this is all new to her. Her hesitant fingers, asking for direction.

Asking me to teach her. God help me. Teach her. I can think of a hundred things I'd like to teach her because I'm the goddamned whore, not her.

So why did she sell herself?

I guess people will do anything for money. Maybe I can't relate because I've always had it. I was born with it, earned more of it. I've never had to make tough choices to get it. I've never been desperate. Is she desperate? I turn my head and watch her sleep. Her hair smells like my shampoo.

How many women have wanted me for the money? Enough of them that paying for sex felt like the most honest way to conduct a relationship. Which is how I got here, isn't it?

What the fuck am I supposed to do with her for thirty days?

I thought this setup was for one night and then Vince told me to have her back in thirty days like she's a rental car. Have her back where? She has a job, a real job, working for me at the Windsor. Is she planning on doing this side job again after me? Taking another... client? Is her cut of five hundred grand not enough for whatever it is she needs? Fucking money. I need to have Canon look into her and find out what kind of debt she has. It can't possibly be insurmountable. If the five hundred didn't already take care of it I'll pay off the rest. Except—that's crazy. She's not mine to take care of. She's temporary. This is temporary. Yet I'm curious.

I wonder what her cut is.

I wonder how much more she needs.

I wonder if it's too soon to fuck her again.

's likely sore. I think? Fucking virgins, hell. Why did I ask her to tell me what it felt like? I'll torture myself replaying her words in my head for the rest of my life. *Like you're breaking me, but also like I might like it. I'm glad I'm doing this with you. Sorry, I'm not any good at dirty talk.*

Jesus. Christ.

I need to get away from her. I toss the covers off, intent on hitting the hotel gym until I've blown off enough steam to keep myself from rutting into Lydia like an animal. I'm dressed, out the door, and on a treadmill in the gym in fewer than seven minutes, one of the benefits of living in a hotel. The gym is empty when I arrive. It'll likely stay empty since the hotel hasn't opened yet and there are fewer than twenty employees living on site—and I'm not expecting to see any of them in the hotel gym this early on a Sunday.

I pick a treadmill and run until I'm covered in sweat, increasing the incline and the speed in an attempt to clear my mind by exhausting my body. Thirty days. When's the last time I fucked the same woman for a month? It's a rhetorical thought because I know exactly when the last time was—and I know it's not been recent. I know my sex life has become a conveyer belt of variety. I know I've been able to fuck nearly any woman I've wanted—and I've wanted.

Lydia assumed she should leave last night. I've not had a single woman stay overnight since I moved to Vegas, so her assumption that I'd want her to get the hell out was correct. It also irritated the shit out of me because I didn't want her to leave—which only served to irritate me further.

I run half a mile, doing nothing but watch each tenth of a mile update on the treadmill's smart screen while running through the upcoming week in my head. Mentally checking my to-do list and searching for something I might have missed. Zoning, permits, staffing, entertainment, food, liquor. Electricity. I had to sit through a meeting about the fucking electric last week because I had to be updated on the contingency plans in the event of an outage. In the event that two separate backup systems failed, did we have a plan, and did I have a rudimentary understanding of the fucking plan should it ever need to be implemented?

I do now.

I watch another half mile go by in tenth-of-a-mile increments.

I'm the one in charge here, I remind myself. It's not as if I have to keep her for the entire thirty days. I could be done today if I wanted—I cut that thought off as soon as it begins. As if I'm not going to fuck her again? Please. I'll fuck her again today, several times likely. But I can see her as much or as little as I want over the next month, is the point. I'm the customer. I'm the one who paid. I'm the one in control here. I'll send her home today. Later today. When I want her again I'll ask her to meet me in my suite after work—and I shouldn't feel a fucking thought over that because I paid her for the use of her time and her body on my schedule.

I run another two miles until I've bought myself enough exhaustion to not think about fucking Lydia again—at least before lunch—then towel my face off as I walk back to my suite. When I walk in she's dressed and sitting on the sofa twiddling her thumbs. Legit twiddling, sitting and twisting her fingers around in her lap. No cell phone. No television. Just sitting there. Her bag is next to her on the sofa, zipped close and waiting as if she's ready to go. It's all fucking weird.

"What are you doing?" I've got a kitchen in this unit. A mostly unused kitchen, but fully equipped, the fridge loaded with mostly beverages. It's open to the living area so I walk in and grab a cold water from the fridge then lean against the countertop and watch her while I down half the bottle in one gulp.

She unclasps her hands and smooths them over her knees before speaking. "I wasn't sure if it was okay for me to leave or not."

Of course she wasn't. Because I paid her to be here. And also because I'm such a dick I didn't leave a note before going to the gym.

"Have you been waiting long?"

"Um, a little bit." She bounces her knee before speaking again. Is she nervous? Do I make her nervous or is it just the situation? "My phone died and I don't have the charger. And I couldn't figure out how to work your TV. It was stuck on some basketball game and I couldn't figure out how to change it so I was just waiting," she finishes with another bounce of her knees and another smoothing of her palms against the denim.

"What do you normally do on Sundays?" I ask, suddenly curious. Curious about what she'd be doing right now if I wasn't a dick and she wasn't sitting in my apartment bored out of her mind waiting on me.

"Oh." She blinks, seeming surprised by the question. "Normal stuff. Laundry or lying by the pool. I'd get an iced coffee from Del Taco or go to the Goodwill."

"What's the Goodwill?"

"A store."

"Okay. I'll take a shower and then we'll go," I say nonchalantly while tossing the empty bottle into the kitchen recycling bin. Maybe if I can learn more about her, learn what she spends money on, I can figure her out. Maybe she has a Goodwill store card with a huge balance. Maybe I can figure out why I care so much, why I'm so fucking curious when it comes to her. "We need to go pick up your stuff anyway," I add, because I've just had an even better idea.

"What stuff?" Her knees stop bouncing and her fingertips freeze over her kneecaps.

"Your stuff. Clothes and shit? Whatever you're going to need."

"Need for what? Today?" Her eyebrows have drawn together in concern or confusion or both.

"For the month. You're staying here."

"What?" She looks a bit aghast at the idea of living with me for an entire month and I can't help but feel a bit offended. I could name at least twenty strippers who'd happily stay here for a month. I'm weighing that thought when she speaks again. "Like staying staying? Like living here? No one said anything about—"

"You should probably read the fine print before making a deal with the devil, Lydia," I interrupt her and I'm a bit more snappish than I'd intended. I shake my head, annoyed with myself and with her even though it's unreasonable, then close the distance between us and snap up the remote. I turn on the TV and flip it to regular cable and then hand it to Lydia, telling her I'll be back in twenty minutes. I can be ready in seven but I need the extra time to jerk off in the shower because after watching her bounce her knees and nervously pick at her jeans, I'm hard again.

When I return Lydia's curled up on the couch, her legs tucked beneath her as she watches a home decorating show. She glances at me as I approach, running her eyes up and down me in a way that's obvious yet I suspect she's completely oblivious to the fact that she's so openly ogling.

"Do you have a DVR?" she asks, turning back to the show. "I'm dying to see how this renovation turns out. Maybe you could record it for me?" She turns her eyes back to me, big green eyes wide with optimism and faith that I might happily take care of this one small thing for her. She drops her chin a fraction and blinks, a hint of doubt covering her face as if she's asked too much. A rogue strand of hair falls across one cheekbone and it makes her seem entirely too real to be anywhere near me.

I pick up the remote and set up a series recording for her as she stands and slips her bag over her shoulder. She's wearing a t-shirt that says 'I love Jesus and tacos.' *Jesus help me with this girl,* is the first thought that comes to my mind and a smile tugs at the corner of my mouth.

"That's what you brought to wear home from a night of debauchery?" I ask, nodding at her shirt with a laugh as I power off the TV and toss the remote onto the couch.

She looks at her shirt and back to me, and I've made her uncomfortable, I see that immediately. "I didn't know." She fidgets with the straps of her bag as she speaks. "I didn't know if I was staying or—I don't know. I didn't know," she says quietly.

I've made her insecure about a t-shirt. *Way to go, asshole.*

"It's funny," I toss out as I open the door for her and we head out to my car. We're on the Strip heading towards Tropicana Avenue before I bring it up again.

"So tacos?" I ask her.

"What?"

"You must really like tacos."

"I guess so. But who doesn't like tacos?"

Fair point.

"And Jesus. You like Jesus too," I add and immediately wonder how in the hell I ever got laid without paying for it. I sound like a fucking idiot.

"I guess so," she mumbles but her head is buried in her phone, working again now that it's attached to the charger in my car.

"How are you feeling today?" I ask so I can change the subject.

"Feeling?" she questions, turning in her seat to face me. We're at the corner of Las Vegas Boulevard and Tropicana, waiting to make a left. "Like emotionally or physically? What do you want to know?" The turn signal clicks like a tiny time bomb in the ensuing silence while I try to gauge her mood. I side-eye her and decide it wasn't a trick question, that she's genuinely waiting for me to clarify.

"Physically," I answer. "Are you good?" Was I too aggressive with her last night? "Are you sore?"

Because if you're not you will be before the day is over.

"I'm okay," she says. But she answers with a tiny shrug of her shoulder which tells me I'm missing something.

"You're okay but what?"

"But nothing." She turns back to her phone and replies to a text.

I make the turn onto Tropicana and drum my fingers on the steering wheel, annoyed. Annoyed with her for holding back and annoyed with myself for caring. What does it matter?

"I don't think you can help," she adds. "It's embarrassing. Forget I said anything." She fidgets in the passenger seat. "I didn't actually say anything though. It's just girl stuff. Forget it."

I give a slight nod of my head and remain silent. Okay then.

"I'm kinda wet," she blurts out when I'm stopped at another stoplight on Tropicana.

Fuck me.

"Not wet like I want to have sex right now, wet like I think you're still dripping out of me from yesterday. Which is so weird and nothing anyone taught me about in high-school sex education and I was worried about—I don't know what I was worried about. But I looked it up and it turns out that it's fairly normal and can last anywhere from a minute till a day after sex and there's no real rhyme or reason to it. It was just, you know, I didn't know and so it freaked me out for a minute but I'm fine now."

Fuck me, that's hot.

"The light is green, Rhys."

I clear my throat and accelerate the car.

"You might as well get used to it because I'm going to fuck you every day."

"Really?" The question is laced with genuine surprise. "You won't be too busy?"

"I'll squeeze you in."

"Oh. Okay, cool."

I take a right in a Del Taco parking lot and merge into the drive-thru lane.

"We're getting Del Taco for real?" Lydia's eyes light up as if I've taken her to a champagne brunch.

"It's your Sunday," I tell her and I wonder how in the fuck this became her Sunday. I was a no. I was a firm no on the twenty-two-year-old from the bar.

The twenty-two-year-old working for my company. The twenty-two-year-old who I knew would be trouble for me.

Firm. Fucking. No.

"What do you want?" I ask her as I inch the car forward, thinking about what a loaded question that is. How did I go from firm no to paying half a million for the pleasure of her company? How? Fuck my life. I'm so distracted with the grand opening looming I can't see straight.

"Ohhh," she says while drumming her hands against her knees as if this is a very exciting decision. "A small iced coffee and an egg and cheese breakfast burrito." She sits back in the passenger seat a moment and crosses her arms, her knees bouncing on the floorboard of my car. "Wait, no," she says, shaking her head. "I want two egg and cheese breakfast burritos. I'm starving. I think I burned a lot of calories last night."

I place her order times two, handing the food to her as it's passed to me through the drive-up window. Then I slide the car into an empty spot in the parking lot, leaving it running. Lydia hands me a burrito before unwrapping straws for both of us and inserting them into the plastic cups, settled in my cup holders.

"Can I ask you something?" she asks as she pulls a burrito from the bag for herself.

"Sure." I take a bite of the one she handed to me. It's not terrible.

"Since you asked me," she adds and I wonder what I asked her. She peels the wrapper back on her burrito before continuing, "What did it feel like? Having sex with me?" She takes a bite of her own burrito and emits a little hum of happiness as the food hits her tongue.

"It felt pretty fucking great." I watch her chew, oddly fascinated with this girl.

"Really?"

"Really."

She takes another bite, being careful not to spill, and watches me, silent. I take a sip of the iced coffee and wince, dropping it back into the cup holder in my car.

"That's not great," I tell her and watch her eyes widen in surprise then narrow in judgment, her right eyebrow raised in challenge. "Too sweet," I protest.

"You're crazy." She rolls her eyes and takes another careful bite of her burrito. I finish off my second and put the car into reverse. I'm taking a right back onto Tropicana when she speaks again.

"I gave you a lot more than that. When you asked," she points out, not incorrectly. She'd been turned towards me while we ate, but she finishes her first burrito and settles back into her seat again, facing forward while digging into the bag for her second.

I slide my sunglasses on to block the intrusions. The sun, her questions, my thoughts. It helps for one out of three.

"Was that a weird question?" she asks as we get stopped by the light on Spencer less than half a minute after pulling back onto Tropicana. "Do people not ask each other that? You asked me so I thought..." She stops speaking, a tiny sigh coming from her lips. "Never mind. I'm so bad at this."

"Humbling," I finally say when the light turns green. "It felt humbling to be inside of you. And wet. Slick and warm and tight. Soft, perfect. You felt fucking perfect, every inch of you. Your tight pussy, the pressure of your fingertips on my arms when it was too tight for you, the scrape of your nails down my sides when it felt just right. When you orgasmed it felt even tighter, and wetter, like your pussy was milking my cock, which made me feel even bigger and harder and like I might lose the circulation to my dick but it'd have been worth it."

Different. It'd felt different in a way that confused me, but made me want more at the same time. Real and raw. Primal.

"So, pretty normal?"

"Yeah, pretty normal."

TWENTY-ONE

RHYS

WE MAKE IT THROUGH a couple of traffic lights and pass a Wal-Mart when I spot a sign for Goodwill and pull into the shopping plaza.

"Oh, my God, we're really going to Goodwill?" The question is asked with way less excitement than I was expecting. I thought I'd get Del Taco excitement but her response was more trepidation than thrill.

"You said this is what you do," I reply, confused.

"I don't think Goodwill is what you think it is and it's really not going to be your thing. I don't even need anything today so we don't have to do this."

I ignore her and park. She grabs her iced coffee with a small groan and opens the car door.

"'Retail store and donation center,'" I read from the sign once I've met her at the bumper of my car. "We're at a thrift shop?"

She hesitates, the toe of her sneaker dragging across the pavement and her body half turned back towards the car. "You're way too busy for this, Rhys. I really don't need to go today. Let's just leave."

"We're already here." I motion to the doors and start walking knowing she'll follow—mostly because I've already locked the car. When I get to the door I

169

hold it open for her and then follow her inside.

Used shit. That's my first thought upon entry. This is not the source of her debt. Lydia has raised the cup of iced coffee to her lips and is taking a long sip, the straw pressed tightly between her lips. I wonder why we're in a thrift shop instead of back at the hotel with my dick between her lips but coming here was my idea. I think. She's standing on one foot, the toe of the other again pivoting on the ground, this time on linoleum instead of asphalt, and now that we're inside the dread on her face has given way to a look of anticipation.

"The color of the week is blue. I always get lucky with blue," she says and I wonder if I'm having a stroke of some kind because nothing, not one thing about the last twenty or so hours makes any sense.

Lydia grabs a cart and drives it towards the back of the store, past industrial shelving set up with piles of crap. I watch her make a quick scan of the shelves as she passes, but clearly she's got some kind of strategy or destination already in mind because she keeps moving, even when an orange ceramic lamp in the shape of a cat catches her eye. It's missing a shade and it's hideous. I'm still staring at it wondering what would have possessed anyone to buy it in the first place, wondering if it was mass-produced or if it's a godawful one-off, when I see Lydia has reached her destination. She's placing a used sheet into the cart when I catch up. A used sheet that looks like it came from the home of a Vegas entertainer circa the fifties.

"When is Vince paying you?" I ask, because I cannot understand what is happening right now. Is she this hard up for money? The sheets aren't labeled as far as I can see so how does she know if they'll fit her bed? I don't think she even got a fitted sheet, just one random top sheet with a shady unknown past.

Which I can't even judge because she's sleeping with me and I don't doubt that my dick has a shadier past than this sheet.

"What?" She stops, and looks at me. She's holding a pants hanger with a pillowcase dangling from the clips, running the material through her fingertips with her other hand.

"When is Vince paying you?" I prod. "Do you need money?"

"Oh." She blinks and drops her eyes from mine, a flicker of hurt or discomfort crossing her face. "I don't know." And then after a pause, "No. I don't want any more of your money. Thank you."

What does she mean she doesn't know? That fucker made me wire him the money before we left, as if I wasn't good for it. Asshole.

"So you didn't get it last night?"

"No. We have to figure out something about taxes first."

Something about taxes? I roll that through my head and I'm sure my face conveys my confusion because she stops, her hand hovering over the rack of pillowcases, and turns to me. "Sorry, is that not a part of your fetish? Should I not have mentioned the taxes?"

"What fetish?"

"Um, the paying for sex thing. I'm not sure how you normally do it. Is it the actual sight of cash that turns you on? Because if you want to leave a pile of money on the nightstand every morning I can slip it back into your nightstand when you're not looking and then you can put it back on my nightstand after you come. Whatever you need."

Do you want to know what the oddest part of that speech was? I don't think she's fucking with me. Not one tiny bit. There wasn't an ounce of reprobation in her tone, just blunt acceptance.

"It's not really a fetish, Lydia. More of a convenience. Like two-day shipping." Fuck me. Did I really just compare her to the convenience of getting a stick of deodorant delivered in under forty-eight hours? I'm not emotionally equipped for her. She's a deep-emotional-attachment kind of girl, not a minimal-expectations kind of girl.

"Oh, okay." She blinks a few times and drops a pillowcase into the cart. "I can be convenient."

"Great." I'm annoyed with this entire conversation and I'm not sure why.

"Great," Lydia replies and I don't get the sense that she's annoyed about anything at all. She takes another sip of her iced coffee and smiles at me around the straw and I want to kiss her. Or fuck her. Or take her back to Vince and forget this entire thing ever happened. That's what she said yesterday, didn't she? *Just take me back. Just take me back, Rhys.*

Take her back to Vince? To Double Diamonds? When the hell did she get involved with him to begin with?

When did this get so convoluted?

I've got responsibilities. A hotel to open. A legacy to build. I'm too goddamned busy for complications right now. Which is why I pay for strippers and lap dances and blow jobs and sex. Which is why I gave half a million to a girl putting an orange cat lamp into a shopping cart right now.

Fuck my fucking life.

I'm under too much stress, I decide. Stress Lydia is going to help me relieve for the next month. Whatever this thing we have is will be out of my system by then. That thought eases some of the tension from my shoulders and I put the rest of it out of my mind.

It seems Lydia's done shopping with the addition of the lamp—a lamp I can only assume is a joke—so once she pays eleven dollars and seventy-four cents for her purchase we leave. She mentions something about what a great find the lamp was as I unlock the car. I don't reply because I haven't a clue what the fuck she's talking about.

She's quiet on the way to her place save for asking if she can have the rest of my coffee. She seems pretty content with the silence, happily sipping away on her second coffee between giving me directions to her place. I already know that she lives near Hennigan's but I don't let on, instead following her directions to take the 515 towards Henderson without comment.

When we exit the highway onto Galleria she starts talking. Sort of.

"The thing is," she starts and then stops, digging the straw around in the cup to distribute the ice or procrastinate, I'm not sure which.

"What's the thing?" I prompt.

"The thing is I didn't know this was a month-long thing," she says. "I know I made a deal with the devil and it's my problem not your problem, blah blah."

Blah blah. That's one way of looking at it.

"But I'm not sure what you're expecting of me."

"I'm expecting you to be available when I want to have sex."

"I mean, yeah. I got that. That's pretty much the

job description, duh."

"Did you just duh me?"

"Sure did."

"You're a terrible hooker."

"I know!" She slaps her palm onto her knee and turns towards me in her seat. "I cannot believe you paid so much for someone with no references or experience. It's not even logical! You're the one giving me a sexual education and you're paying me for the privilege. You should really work on your negotiation skills, because I think Vince hosed you." She finishes that speech with a little shake of her head before continuing. "I don't think buying me was a sound financial purchase. I bet your financial advisor is going to be very disappointed when he finds out."

I glance over at her to gauge if she's serious right now. My guess is one hundred percent serious.

"I'm sure Anthony will manage his disappointment accordingly."

"Maybe he can find a way to put me on your taxes as an expense. Like the swag. Filed under grand opening entertainment or something? I'm sure Vince will give you a receipt, right? If he invoices this as entertainment it wouldn't be a lie. Sex in and of itself is sort of entertaining."

My certainty about if she's fucking with me or not just dropped to eighty percent so I keep my mouth shut, which she takes as an invitation to keep talking. I miss quiet Lydia. I enjoyed her for the five minutes I knew her.

"It would be one thing if you were terrible at sex and you needed to pay someone to fake having a good time, but you're super-good at sex! I didn't have to fake anything."

"Thank you," I deadpan in reply.

"Oh, shoot, was that rude? I bet you're good at other stuff too. You must be, you're very successful. I bet you're good at CEOing stuff."

"Besides negotiating."

"Yeah," she says with a small sigh. "Besides that. But you know, you're probably just not thinking clearly right now, what with the grand opening just around the corner. I'm sure you're a much better negotiator when you're not under so much stress. But it's fine because you're good at so many other things, like working out and making your own bed and recycling." She's counting off on her fingers as she rattles my accomplishments off, pausing after the third finger. "And sharing. You're an excellent sharer." She jiggles the iced coffee with one hand and holds up a fourth finger on the other. "And—" She pauses again, clearly having run out of accomplishments she can praise me for, which vaguely disappoints me. It also makes me wonder what sorts of accomplishments might impress her enough to win her respect. "Did you by chance have anything to do with the coffee machine in the break room? Because it's phenomenal."

"What was the thing, Lydia? To begin with? Remind me why we're having this conversation?"

"Oh! Right. The thing is I didn't realize this was for a month so I only purchased one set of sexy underwear. My regular stuff is all cotton bikini bottoms. Not even thongs 'cause I prefer underwear that covers my butt."

The idea of Lydia with a drawer full of boring cotton panties that she doesn't expect anyone to see has me hard again. Maybe there's something wrong with my cock? Like some kind of stress-induced permanent semi-hard-on? That doesn't sound right.

"And I don't have any sexy pajamas either. So I'm not sure what you expect me to pack. That's what I was trying to ask you about expectations. I got the sex part, I'm just not sure what you expect from me the other twenty-three and a half hours a day."

"Last night was a hell of a lot longer than half an hour," I gripe as we hit another stoplight.

"I know! I'm sorry! But you kept going down on me and kissing me and doing all those things that were not putting your penis inside of me. I don't think that article I read was counting all that other stuff when they came up with that seven- to thirteen-minute average and I didn't know yet about that other stuff or how long you'd want to do it."

I'm going to need Jesus to take the wheel of this car if she doesn't shut up soon.

"Anyway, we can be quicker, I'm sure. I know you're busy so maybe we can have a couple of quickies and that will bring our average down. Like if we have sex a couple times for five minutes and one time for an hour, then that's an average of like twenty or twenty-five minutes per sexing. Shoot, is that still too long? Maybe three quickies for every long one? You're the one with a schedule so it's up to you."

Jesus. Wheel. I adjust my cock as she continues chatting away.

"Anyway, that wasn't really my point," she says, taking a breath.

Thank fuck for small favors.

"My point was that I don't have any sexy stuff but I can run out and buy some today. I just need to know what you're into because that stuff is expensive and you didn't seem that impressed with the negligee thing and I'm not a mind reader."

The negligee thing she was wearing on stage in front of other men. She's right about that. I hated it.

"Just pack whatever you'd normally wear, Lydia."

"Whatever I normally wear is not what you think it is, Rhys. Are you sure you don't want me to run out and get some stuff? Or I could ask my new friend Staci for help. She could probably tell me where to order online if you're into something a little more hardcore than what I can find at the Fashion Show mall. Do you want me in leather or netting or dressed like a pony or something? Just tell me."

She brings the straw to her lips and takes another sip, blinking at me in innocent curiosity and without a hint of judgment.

"I want you exactly the way you are."

"Oh." A tiny line furrows her brow as if this is confusing to her. Or perhaps she was hoping I was into bondage or some shit, it's hard to tell with her.

"Were you hoping to experience something extreme, Lydia? Did you want me to get you a butt plug with a tail and ask you to crawl around my apartment? Pierce your nipples? Paddle you?"

"Not particularly, no. I just want to be good for you. I like it when you tell me I'm a good girl. That really does it for me."

"Does it?"

"Mmm-hmm," she murmurs and wiggles in her seat.

I tell her I need some quiet time after that.

The complex she lives at is nice. An upscale development just twenty minutes from the Strip, close enough to be convenient but far enough to have a relaxed residential feel. She lives in a unit near the clubhouse which must have a gym, as some sweat-covered asshole passes us on his way out. He calls out a "Hey, Lydia," as he passes, which pisses me the fuck off.

"Friend of yours?" I question as I trail behind her to her door, carrying the orange cat lamp.

"I met him at the pool once," she says, flashing me a chagrined smile over her shoulder. "But I can't remember his name so I'm always just like 'Hey, you!' when he tries to talk to me."

I'd tell her that he wouldn't give a shit about reminding her what his name is if she'd be willing to give him the time of day, but fuck that. I'm not paying her to give her tips on picking up other men.

She unlocks her apartment door and calls out for her roommate, who doesn't appear to be home.

"Weird, I thought she was here," Lydia says. She looks sad about missing her. "I guess I'll see her tomorrow," she says with a shrug.

"Are you close?" I ask for lack of anything else to talk about.

"She's my best friend."

"Have you known her long?"

"A couple of years. We met in college, then we both got hired at the Windsor so we decided to move here together and be roommates."

"Ah." I hadn't realized her roommate was an employee too, but it makes sense. I know we did a lot of hiring at college job fairs. Fuck, I hate the reminder that Lydia was in college so recently.

"I'll take this," she says, taking the lamp from my hand. I'd forgotten I was even holding the hideous thing. She disappears into one of the bedrooms so I take stock of her apartment. I think this is a relatively new development. The apartment itself isn't huge but the floor plan is open and the appliances look new. The couch looks new, along with the end tables and lamps. Normal lamps, I note, not shaped like a cat or a unicorn or whatever the fuck else she's into. There's an old dresser that's been painted teal being used to hold the television and a kitchen table with mismatched chairs that I suspect came from Goodwill. There's a sash of some kind hanging from a cork board near the kitchen table. Like a pageant sash, but uglier. I walk closer to check it out as Lydia calls out from the bedroom that she's packing normal stuff.

This sash is even more ridiculous than the lamp. There's something called a bar badge sewn onto it. And a dating app badge. And a confidence badge. Pinned to the bulletin board but not sewn onto the sash is a Rhys badge. And a sex badge. And a butt stuff badge.

My cock throbs at the idea of taking Lydia's ass but my mind is stuck on the Rhys badge. Am I some kind of a game to her?

The front door opens and Payton appears. I step away from the bulletin board as Lydia pops out of her room with a happy exclamation over her friend's arrival. She introduces us and then pauses, taking a second glance at her friend.

"Payton, why are you still wearing the same thing you had on last night?"

"Um," Payton replies, glancing down at herself as if in confusion. "Am I? Enough about me. How was the sex last night?"

"Payton!" Lydia's eyes widen and she shoots me a look, her expression mortified. "I'm not going to tell you what Rhys is like in bed when he's standing right here."

"Okay, so tomorrow at lunch?" Payton seems

totally nonplussed over Lydia's rebuttal. Lydia's eyes dart back and forth between me and Payton.

"Probably not then either, Payton."

"Ohhh," Payton drawls, looking between us. "Of course not. We'd never discuss such a thing. Wink, wink."

She actually says 'wink, wink' out loud.

"Are you almost ready? I've got a lot of work to get done this afternoon." Including giving Lydia multiple orgasms so they're fresh on her mind when she recaps it during her lunch. Because impressing this virgin has somehow, inexplicably, become my thing.

TWENTY–TWO

RHYS DISAPPEARS INTO his home office almost as soon as we return to the hotel. Besides his bedroom and the room he's using as an office there's a spare bedroom, but Rhys places my suitcase in his room and tells me to unpack. So I do. I line up my shampoo and conditioner next to his in the shower. I hang my clothes next to his in the closet and I pretend this is all normal and that he likes me. Likes me a girlfriend amount, not a hooker amount, which is ridiculous because no one moves their girlfriend in after one date.

I check the fridge and find it empty save for bottled water, craft private-label beer from Hennigan's, orange juice, a carton of eggs and a bottle of mustard. There's a basket of fresh fruit on the counter so I help myself to a pear and then stare at the view of the Vegas Strip while I eat it.

After that I've officially run out of things to do and I think it's been all of half an hour since I got here so I doubt Rhys is emerging from his office anytime soon. So I resort to my normal Sunday afternoon activity: pajamas and home renovation shows on cable. I'm in my favorite pair of sheet pajama pants and a tank top, sprawled out on Rhys's couch waiting to find out which house a couple from Downers Grove, Illinois chooses on their house hunt, when the front door opens and Canon walks in.

"Oh, hey, I didn't realize you were here," he says, spotting me halfway to the bedroom Rhys has his office set up in. I'm slumped on the couch with my feet on the coffee table and my phone in my hand playing a word game while I wait to find out if location trumps yard space for the Illinois couple. "Have you moved in?" Canon asks with a wide grin, eyeing the way I'm sprawled on the sofa in pajamas.

"Basically," I say, shrugging my shoulder as if I've got no idea how this happened either. Mostly I avert my gaze because he just saw me yesterday wearing a sheer nightie auctioning my virginity and that is super-embarrassing.

"Wow. This is so much better than I anticipated," he says, laughing to himself as he continues down the hall to find Rhys.

The Illinois couple picks the house with the good yard and the outdated kitchen. I score thirty-four points spelling the word 'jeed.' I don't even know what that word means. I mostly just move the letters around until I get a word worth a decent number of points and then I hit play.

Rhys and Canon emerge from the office, Canon telling us to have a good night, and then he's gone. Rhys flips the safety deadbolt as the door closes, walks over to where I'm sitting and stops.

"Dinner?"

Oh.

"You want me to get dressed?" I toss the blanket off of myself and place my feet on the floor and stand. Getting redressed on a Sunday is so not my idea of a good time.

"No, we'll eat here."

"Eat what? You don't have any food." I drop back onto the sofa with my blanket, relieved I don't have to get dressed.

"We'll order from the kitchen. What do you want?"

"Do you order all your meals from the kitchen?"

"Pretty much," he says like this isn't a weird thing. I wonder how I'm going to make it without Del Taco. I bet I can get Payton to bring me an iced java coffee on her way to work. "What do you want?" He's walked over to the kitchen and picked up some kind of smart screen device that I saw earlier on a charging dock next to the stove. The stove that still had the instruction manual inside of it.

"I don't know. What do they have? Do you have a menu?"

"They have whatever you want."

"Whatever I want?"

"Yes."

"So I could order..." I search my brain for something really outlandish and come up totally blank. Surely they can make a cheeseburger or a pepperoni pizza or a chicken salad or a turkey sandwich. "I could order lemon pie for dinner and they'd bring it?"

"I have no idea how long it would take but yes, they'd bring it. Did you want lemon pie?" He's tapping on the screen and I hope he's not just ordered me a lemon pie because I don't actually like lemon pie. It was just the wildest thing I could come up with on short notice, which is really really lame.

"What are you having?"

"Grilled chicken, a baked potato and broccoli."

"Oh! I know what I want." I'm sort of excited now because this is my favorite thing ever, but making it myself requires buying so many ingredients that it's really not cost-effective. He raises his brow in question so I continue. "I'd like a salad with shredded chicken, corn, black beans, avocado, tomatoes, cheese and cilantro lime dressing on the side."

Rhys taps in my order. "No pie?"

"Err, no. I was joking about the pie." I say it super-casually, like a girl who would never order pie. But the idea of a magical kitchen where I can order anything is too much temptation. "Do they have birthday-cake-flavored ice cream?"

"Isn't that just vanilla?"

"No! No, it's not just vanilla." I huff and shake my head. "You're really sheltered, Rhys. You've been alive twelve whole years longer than I have yet there's so much you still don't know."

Rhys stares at me over the tablet without speaking then shakes his head as if he's snapping himself out of his thoughts.

"If they don't someone will run out and get it," he says as he finishes tapping our order in before tossing the device onto the sofa.

"This is some life you've got here," I tell him. "Housekeeping. Room service. Killer views."

"It's something," he says, dropping onto the sofa beside me and pulling my legs into his lap. I freeze for a moment because it's such a weird couplish thing to do, but Rhys doesn't seem to notice, his attention on the television. "What are we watching?"

We.

I've never been a we. I've always wanted to be one, even in high school when I was too busy and too shy to do much of anything about it. I remember during my junior year, the Monday after a dance I hadn't attended, another girl looked at me in the hallway and said, "Oh, look, there's that girl who couldn't get a date to the dance."

She was a sophomore, someone I only knew in passing, but her words devastated me for—well, for a long time. But here I am, with the most attractive man I've ever laid eyes on, lying on his couch with my legs in his lap while we wait for room service.

So what if it's fake? It could be real. It feels sorta real. Rhys starts massaging the arches of my feet and that feels pretty real. Unless he's got a foot fetish and I've finally cracked his code.

"*House Hunters*," I finally answer.

"What is *House Hunters*?"

I stare at him, unsure if he's joking or not. He's not. "You don't know what *House Hunters* is?"

"Nope."

"It's been on for like a hundred seasons."

"A hundred?"

"At least. You are the only person in the universe who hasn't seen *House Hunters*. You really need to live a little, Rhys."

"So what is it I'm missing?"

"Okay, so every episode features a couple buying a house. In a different city in the United States. Unless you're watching *House Hunters International* and then they could be buying a house anywhere! Like Paris or Prague or Edinburgh or Heidelberg."

"Heidelberg?"

"It's in Germany. You'd know that if you watched *House Hunters International*." I'm more than a little smug about my knowledge of a random city in Europe.

"I know where Heidelberg is."

Oh.

"Why is watching someone look for a house interesting?"

"How is it not?" Rhys laughs at the expression on my face but I really don't get how he's not getting this. "Every couple has a different budget, different priorities, in a different city. And you get to see what kind of house they can buy for that budget in that city. They view three homes and then they pick one. But before they pick they recap all three and you guess which one they're going to pick."

"Uh-huh."

"It's very interesting. You'll see."

"Couldn't you just look up some houses on Zillow and save yourself twenty-five minutes?"

"Pffft. That's not the same."

"Okay." Rhys nods. "So what city are we watching now?" His thumbs continue to knead the bottom of my foot and this might be the most blissful moment of my life. Well, second. Those orgasms he gave me last night definitely rank first.

"You, my friend, are in for a special treat."

"Am I?" His lips quirk in amusement. He can be as amused as he likes because he has no idea how lucky he's about to be. "These are nice, by the way," he says, fingering the material of my pajama pants. I'm still not sure if he's serious about this 'wear what I'd normally wear' nonsense so I keep the fact that I made these pants out of an old sheet to myself.

"You are. Up next is an episode of *House Hunters Renovation*. Which means we get to see them pick their house and renovate it. Whew!" I fan myself with my hand like I need to cool down. I'm joking. A little bit. It is my favorite of the *House Hunters*.

We're halfway through the episode—a couple in Austin, Texas have selected their house and renovations are just beginning—when our food arrives. Rhys gets up to get the door and a guy from food and beverage wheels in a cart exactly like they do in the movies. It's probably exactly like they do it in real life too but I've never had room service before. I've been on plenty of family vacations with my dads, but room service was never a thing we did.

The guy from food and beverage is an older gentleman named Mitchell. He was in one of my orientation groups a couple of weeks back and I know he recognizes me as he's moving the trays to the island countertop in the kitchen per Rhys' direction because he says, "Good evening, Miss Clark."

"Hi, Mitch." I wave from the couch. "How has your day been so far?"

"No complaints. We're not too busy what with the hotel not being officially open yet. Suspect that's about to change real quick."

"It better," Rhys agrees. He escorts Mitchell to the door and then tells me he's putting my ice cream in the freezer.

"Okay. I hope there's room in there," I tease.

"Oh, you think you're funny, don't you?"

"You have a full-size top-of-the-line refrigerator filled with water and ketchup, so yes."

He places our food on the coffee table and sits back down beside me and, not for nothing, I see him eyeing the television. He'd never admit it, but I bet he's just as curious as I am if that kitchen wall can come down easily or if the couple from Austin is going to have to spring for an expensive beam.

"So, um, how are we doing this with work?" I ask

him during the next commercial break.

"What do you mean?" He forks a piece of chicken into his mouth. I know this is a little crazy but he's a very sexy chewer.

"I'm sorta living here."

"For a month."

"Or until you get bored with me."

He turns his head and glances at me when I say that, a flicker of something crossing his expression before he turns back to the television.

"I know that Sutton Travel has a fairly liberal fraternization policy," I say, referring to the parent company that owns the Windsor, and trying to guide the conversation back to the issue at hand, "but people are going to see me here, like Mitchell just did. Or see me coming and going or using the executive elevator to get to work in the morning. They're going to assume that I'm your girlfriend, unless you want me to sneak in and out? I could take the elevator down to the parking garage and then walk over to the employee entrance and take that elevator to the fourth floor. That would work." I hold my breath and wonder if this is the moment he realizes he only liked me in a one-night way, not in a month-long way, and tells me to go.

I really like him in a month-long way.

At least.

Maybe even in a several-months way.

I know my liking seems a little presumptuous, a little naive, but you know how some men have that thing? A presence? That thing that sucks the air out of the room when they walk in, when your eyes gravitate towards them even before you should know they're there? That pull isn't normal—it cannot be, because I've met lots and lots of men during my lifetime and I've only ever felt it with Rhys.

I don't know how long that thing lasts. Obviously this is my first time experiencing that thing, but it can't possibly just flip off or extinguish in a month. It's already been a month since the first time I felt it, that first night in the bar when he was with his drunk British friend (who I've since pieced together is the CEO of Sutton Travel and Rhys' cousin, so I should probably stop referring to him as the drunk British friend in case I ever meet him) and the thing is not diminishing. The thing has only gotten stronger. And now I have feelings for him as a person in addition to the thing, which is clearly some kind of voodoo sexual pull.

But maybe this is the moment that Rhys realizes he's not feeling the thing. Maybe at all, or maybe not enough to want me here. Maybe he had his fill of me and that's that. There must be a reason he doesn't have a girlfriend, right? A reason he prefers dancers, strippers, whatever his normal preference is. Maybe he likes the variety.

"No, I don't want you to sneak anywhere. Come and go as you please. I'll take care of the office in the morning."

I poke at a piece of shredded chicken in my salad, which is delicious, way better than when I have to make it myself, and contemplate what 'taking care of it' means. I want to ask questions about that, but he's turned his attention back to the television and his expression didn't really bode well for questioning. Plus I trust him when he says he'll take care of it. The questions are really just for my own nosy interest so I decide to let it drop until tomorrow.

We watch the rest of the episode in silence. The kitchen wall comes down, but it does require a thirty-five-hundred-dollar support beam to make their dream kitchen a reality. Then they get hit with an unexpected roof leak and the contingency budget is blown. It all ends well though, when they find tile for the renovated master bath on clearance and call in a friend to help them lay it themselves in order to stay on budget. The renovation finishes on time and seven thousand dollars over their original eighty-thousand-dollar budget.

"What did you think?" I ask him when the episode ends.

"Hmm," he replies, as if he needs to mull it over. We've finished our dinners and somehow—I really could not explain how it happened—sometime in the last ten minutes of the episode I ended up with my head on Rhys' chest, both of us reclined on the sofa. "What is it about it that appeals to you?" He's running his fingers through the strands of my ponytail and it feels just as good as the mini-foot massage I got earlier. I decide Rhys is good at the touching too. It's very comforting, reassuring in a wordless way. Also, there might be a thirty percent chance I'm falling for him.

"I love seeing what's possible. At first glance that house was so dated and dark. But it was a hidden gem, you know? It just needed the right person to come along and uncover its potential. With just a little bit of effort, relocating the laundry room and renovating the kitchen meant suddenly the house was a bright spacious home the way it was always meant to be."

"A lot of effort is more like it."

"Sometimes the effort is worth it." I say it softly, a bit more to myself than to him. I'm playing with the loop on the waistband of his jeans, running the material between my finger and thumb, my eyes on the television.

"They could have just bought a move-in-ready house and skipped the hassle."

"Maybe. But maybe they really wanted that particular home and none of the move-in-ready homes turned them on." He stills beneath me, his hand pausing in my hair. "Maybe they had a real-estate fetish for that lot or something. Never mind," I finish in a rush. I think my real-estate analogies might be too revealing, yet I can't stop. "Plus every episode has a happily-ever-after."

"A house-hunting happily-ever-after?"

"Yes. It's a very rewarding viewing experience. You know they're going to pick one of the three houses because they always pick one of the three houses. You are virtually guaranteed at the end of each episode one house will be living its best life with a new family."

"What about the two houses that didn't get picked?"

"I don't like to think about them."

"Of course not."

"I'm sure they got picked," I add, after a minute, because it is a bothersome detail. "Off screen. Just because it didn't happen during the episode doesn't mean it never happened for those homes."

"Maybe the other homes were too damaged to deserve a family. Maybe they were filled with mold and needed to be leveled." He's playing with my hair again as he talks.

"Nope. Mold can be remediated. They just needed the right buyer to see their potential."

A new episode starts and Rhys doesn't make any move to get up from the couch. This time it's an episode of *Beach Hunters*, in which prospective homeowners are searching for their dream homes with beach access.

I've never been much of a beach girl.

"Do you have more work left to do tonight?" I ask, glancing up at him under my lashes. I'm not sure how much time I have with him or how to go about asking for what I want.

"Did you want me to get back to work?"

"No." I shake my head against his chest, the fabric from his t-shirt soft against my chin.

"I'm done working for the night."

"That's great."

"Why is that?"

I smooth my open palm against his chest and wonder how I make the sex happen again. "Maybe we can work on our AST," I offer.

"AST?"

"Average sex time. Remember we need to work on our efficiencies because you're so busy."

His eyes close for a moment and a small groan emits from his lips. I can't decipher the groan though. Is it interest? Exasperation? Arousal? I'm not at all sure. I eye the clock, wondering what time he's planning on starting work in the morning. Maybe it's time for him to go to bed, I have no idea.

"We could be quick, to bring the average down," I add in case he's considering skipping half an hour of sleep to have sex. "Or I could give you a blow job. I don't think that would count towards the AST average though. But I think I read something about blow jobs helping with sleep so it would still be a very efficient use of your time, don't you think?"

He expels a breath and his eyes open, looking at me with a sense of bewilderment.

"Have you ever given a blow job, Lydia?"

"No." I shake my head. "I gave an ex-boyfriend a few hand jobs but he came pretty fast without me really doing much. That's why I thought that seven to thirteen minutes was a reasonable goal because it only took that guy like two minutes to come."

Rhys stops playing with my hair and uses that hand to rub at the lines on his forehead so I fear I might be losing his interest.

"I know how to though," I add quickly. "I watched a few videos to get the gist and I'm a quick learner." I've always been proud of my ability to catch on quickly. "I haven't forgotten that you want me to choke on your dick, but you'll have to teach me that part because none of the videos I saw explained if the women were simply born without a gag reflex, or if not, how they were able to overcome it. Also some of them just swallowed the penis without a sound and some of them were very noisy about it and I wasn't sure which you were looking for."

"Lydia." He grits the response between his teeth.

"Yes?"

"Please stop talking."

Oh, snap.

I bite my lip to hide my disappointment. Both over missing out on the sex tonight and wondering where I lost his interest. I run the conversation back through my mind trying to pinpoint exactly where I lost him so I can remove it from my wheelhouse of seduction techniques.

But wait.

He is interested. I know he's interested because I can feel his interest growing against my stomach and it's new interest, it wasn't there during the last ten minutes of the home renovation when I was lying on top of him and the quartz countertops were being revealed. So maybe 'please stop talking' meant 'get to work?' I am here on a job after all. When I was a Girl Trooper our leader Mrs. Barnes used to tell us 'less talking, more working' when we were sorting our cookie orders but I guess that's not really the same thing at all.

Still.

It could be a similar thing.

I move my eyes to his and slide my hand from his chest to his growing interest and apply a bit of pressure. When he doesn't stop me I slide off the couch and settle on my knees between his spread ones and move to unzip him, but he stops me again.

"Lydia, stop. Stand up."

TWENTY-THREE

RHYS

"DID I DO SOMETHING wrong? I didn't even start yet." Lydia looks confused, and possibly disappointed. She's disappointed about being denied encouragement to give me a blow job? Fuck my fucking life. She doesn't stand as I've told her, instead she sits back on her heels and looks up at me, a twinge of hurt in her eyes.

"No, you didn't do anything wrong." I shake my head and pinch the bridge of my nose. Jesus. She's so fucking eager. Eager to please me, and I don't deserve it. I don't deserve her. Even if I did pay for her to be here, pay for her to please me.

"Are you worried I'm going to be bad at it? Because in my mind I'm pretty good at it, but I can't confirm that if I can't try. Plus I want to. I want to try. I want to know what it would feel like to do that for you."

"I'll let you try. Just not tonight."

"Okay, when?"

"Wednesday," I toss out because I've lost my goddamned mind. I don't even know where Wednesday came from, but Lydia is still on her knees in front of me and I don't want to quell her natural enthusiasm for sex and it's not like I don't *want* the blow job. Of course I want it. Fuck.

She rolls her bottom lip between her teeth and then smiles, nodding once as if Wednesday was a reasonable answer to when she can suck my cock. Her palms are flat on her thighs, on top of the cute pajama bottoms she's wearing. Her hair is pulled off her face in a pony tail and I can make out her nipples beneath the tank top and this all seems so normal. So fucking normal having her here, as if she's always been here, as if she was always meant to be here.

I hit the remote, turning off the television, and stand, holding out my hand to pull her up from the floor. She slips her hand into mine and rises up on her knees before moving one foot out from beneath her to stand. When she's up I tug her closer and kiss her. A tiny squeal gets lost in her throat as she clearly wasn't expecting the kiss. Then she leans into me and wraps her arms around my neck to draw me closer. Her nipples are pressed against my chest, her lips softly pliant underneath mine, and her fingers are tugging at the short strands of hair on the back of my neck and this—this is making me rock-hard.

I move my hands to the back of her thighs and lift until she wraps her legs around my waist. It gives me a weird sense of peace as I walk through the living room turning off the lights with Lydia hanging onto me, a fucked-up security in knowing she'll be here all night, knowing she'll still be here in the morning. Why doesn't it feel suffocating? It should, shouldn't it? Yet Lydia's physically hanging on me and I like it. I like having her here. I like the company. I like her and her taco-themed t-shirts and her love of cheap fast food and her weird shopping habits and her glee for watching someone she doesn't even know pick out a house in a city she's never set foot in.

I want to know everything I don't know about her yet. All of it.

I just need to get to the bottom of her involvement with Vince. Whatever it is I can fix it. She's twenty-two fucking years old and thinks thrift-store shopping is fun, how much debt can she possibly be in? Canon's promised me a report by tomorrow. I'll start there.

"We're doing the sex now, right?" She's been kissing the side of my neck as I walked. Rubbing her pelvis against me with her signature dry-hump move. I like that too. I know I shouldn't. I know her eagerness is due to a lack of experience and that lack of experience is somewhat due to her age, and somewhat due to her complete cluelessness about men, but I fucking love that about her. She's not jaded yet. She doesn't know shit about seduction. She blushes when I so much as look at her and she tells me way too much. Like right now. Right now when she bounces in my arms and pulls back just far enough to look me in the eye to ask if we're doing the sex. The doubt from earlier is gone, replaced with bright enthusiasm.

I've had a lot of sex and I'm certain that not one single woman has ever asked me if we're about to do the sex.

"The kissing and your hand on my ass and this progression towards the bedroom means we're going to have sex, right? You're passing on the blow job because you've got time for real sex?" When I don't answer her immediately her eyes widen and then she blinks and says in a much softer voice that might be meant for her, "Please say yes."

"Yes, we're doing the sex, Lydia."

"Yay!"

No one's ever said that to me before either. I've heard every gratuitous compliment in the book while fucking, but never yay. And Jesus help me, I think that's the same yay she reserves for the iced coffee at Del Taco so I know it's genuine.

"Tell me something, Lydia."

"Okay." She tilts her head to the side, all wide eyes and eager anticipation.

"Tell me how you graduated from college still a virgin."

"The thing about that, Rhys," she begins but pauses as if searching for the right words.

"What's the thing?"

"I know this might come as a surprise, so prepare yourself. The thing is I was a bit of a nerd in high school."

"You don't say." I keep a straight face.

"Yeah." She nods. "It's true. And it sorta spilled over into college. I wanted to have sex, I really did. But I wanted to really feel it. Feel the connection. Feel like ripping my clothes off, but I never did. Making out was kinda fun but in an 'I'm good, you can leave your pants on' kind of way."

"So you decided selling it was the route to go?" I ask, confused.

She glances away and bites her bottom lip, a small frown marring her forehead. "The thing about that is, I was turning into a spinster." She glances back at me as if to see what my reaction is.

"A spinster. A twenty-two-year-old spinster?"

"Yup. Can we talk about this later?"

I drop her at the foot of my bed and remove her tank top in one motion. I untie the satin ribbon bow that's holding her pajama bottoms around her waist and remove those from her as well. Then I drop to my knees and lift one of her legs over my shoulder.

"How come you get to do the oral and I have to wait until Wednesday to do the oral?"

"Because I'm in charge and I say so."

"Hmm, I do like you being in charge. Your confidence makes me feel confident. And wanted. And also I just sorta get off on following directions."

Her breathing has increased while she speaks and her chest is flush. She's got small tits. They're real and perfect and I like watching them rise and fall on her chest from this angle. I like watching her head fall back when I suck her clit between my lips and I fucking love the feel of her fingers gripping my shoulders so she doesn't fall over and the way she's tilting her hips to get closer to my mouth.

I grip her ass cheeks with my hands to steady her and slide the tip of my finger over the strip of skin from her pussy to her ass. That gets her attention. Her head falls forward with a small 'oh' coming from her mouth as I circle her asshole with the tip of my finger. She tenses then relaxes when I suck harder on her clit. The heel of her foot digs into my back and she rises up on the ball of her one foot when I circle again.

She's fucking perfect.

I remove her foot from my shoulder and push her back onto the bed so I can spread her legs farther apart. I like unrestricted access while I'm working, though this is more of a hobby than a job.

"Tell me what you like," I instruct as I run my hands up and down the insides of her thighs. I place a kiss on her stomach, just below her belly button, and palm her calves as I position her knees where I want them.

"All yesses so far," she breathes out on a happy sigh and I laugh.

"I meant very specifically, good girl, since you don't have any comparison."

I spread her apart with my thumbs and trail my tongue between her folds while keeping an eye on her. She's got one hand on her stomach and the other gripping the duvet over her head. Her tits are rising and falling on her chest and her head is turned to the side facing the windows, but her eyes are scrunched closed.

Fuck, she's so pretty here. Wet and pink and slick and I'm fucking into it. I could look at her and taste her all night.

I run my tongue over her from bottom to top, lightly. Then again with more force.

"Which did you prefer?"

"Oh." Her eyes blink open and she squirms. "I don't know. I liked it both ways."

I do it again. And once more before she arches her foot and tells me she liked the lighter sweep best.

Then I wrap my mouth over her clit and suck. Softly first. Then again with more suction. She likes the rougher suction here.

I lick and suck and nip and include fingers into the mix, all the while asking her to verbalize which she likes best. I have a pretty good idea of exactly what she likes based on the rise of her chest and the arch of her feet. The way the fingers lying on her stomach tense and relax and how the muscles on her thighs flex and her legs fall open or tighten around my shoulders.

But I like hearing it from her.

"What if I don't like this the same way every time though?" she asks after she's come twice. Her thighs are wet from herself and she's a bit breathless as I've just made her tell me exactly how much pressure she likes from my fingers stroking that perfect spot inside her. "What if I'm teaching you bad habits based on what I'm liking right this second?"

God help me, she's too much.

"I'm much better at adapting than negotiating," I respond. I manage to do it without breaking a smile.

"Oh. Okay." She nods and blows out a breath.

I stand and yank my shirt off with one hand to the back of my neck and a tug. Then I drop my pants and pull Lydia to a standing position before lying back on the bed myself.

"Straddle me," I tell her, fisting my cock with one hand. I'm so fucking hard I feel like I could blow right now. I thumb the pre-cum off my tip and use it to jack myself. Lydia's eyes flare at the instruction and then she's clambering up the bed and tossing one leg over mine, placing her hand on my chest for balance and resting her weight on my thighs with her bottom.

She takes over for me, sliding her hand up and down the length of me, her eyes darting back and forth between my cock and my face, her tongue peeking out between her lips in concentration.

"I still don't get how this fits inside of me," she says, eyes wide as she lifts on her knees a bit to guide me to her entrance.

"It fit nicely last night," I remind her and she blushes.

"My body must produce some kind of magic lubrication to make this possible." She brushes the head of me against her entrance and I hiss at the heat and wetness and it takes a considerable amount of restraint not to take over and slam up into her.

Instead I rub my hands along the tops of her thighs, encouraging her as she notches me inside.

So fucking tight. She might be right about the magic.

She manages to sink an inch or so onto me, but her face is tense and her pussy is tenser. She lifts up and sinks back down, blowing out a breath while I tell her to relax. I touch her everywhere. I stroke her thighs, run my hands up her sides, cup her tits and thumb her nipples all while she exhales and repeats the inch or two descent before rising back up on her knees to stop gravity from doing its job.

"I can't, Rhys. I can't do it like this yet. I'm sorry." She lets go of my cock and swings her leg over and off of me, dropping to her ass on the mattress beside me. "I'm sorry," she repeats and I frown because what the fuck? Hearing 'I'm sorry' coming out of her mouth is the last thing I want right now.

"You're too big and it's too tight that way. I'm not very good at this. It's too soon, I have to work up to doing it like that. It works better for me if you're doing it. Did you pay Vince already? You should ask for a refund or a reduced rate or something since I cannot do it all the ways you want to do it. I'm sorry. Can we do it a different way where you're the doer? Like doggie style maybe? Then you'd be in charge and I'm better at this when you're in charge and on top." She's waving her hands around as she talks and I grab one and pull her down on top of me.

"Lydia." I pause until I know I've got her attention.

"What?"

"I don't want you to be sorry."

"Okay," she agrees but she drops her eyes and her shoulders are still tense.

"We don't have to do a position that makes you uncomfortable. Ever."

"Okay."

"Though I promise you, riding me like a filthy cowgirl is a position you'll enjoy very much when you work up a little confidence."

"Hmm, maybe." She shrugs but she's drawing circles on my chest with her fingertip and peeking at me beneath her lashes, a blush again coloring her skin.

"And until then there are many, many more configurations we can try."

That works.

"How many?" Her interest is piqued and she's wiggled closer. Her eyes are shining at me in that way that makes me feel like I'm the center of the fucking universe.

"So many. But we're going to skip doggie style for now, as lovely as an offer as it was, and as much as I'd like you on your hands and knees while I yank on your hair and pound into you from behind."

"Oh." She pouts, making no effort to hide her expression, her brow furrowed and her lips turned down. "Why can't we do that right now? I like the sound of that."

"Because I can't see your face that way. And I want to see your face while I'm fucking you."

"Ohhh, okay." She draws out the word 'oh.' "I like your face too." Her lips curve into an impish smile. "I like seeing your face all the time though. I'm especially looking forward to seeing your face on Wednesday."

"You," I tell her, then roll us over so she's beneath me, "are quite the minx for such a good girl." I kiss her until she's relaxed and digging a heel into my ass trying to pull me closer. I kneel on the bed and bend her knees up to her chest, keeping her knees and calves together and placing both of her ankles on my left shoulder. Then I sink into her. God, she feels good. I watch her eyes widen and her lips form a tiny o. She blinks rapidly then smiles.

"Oh, wow. I had no idea." She shakes her head against the pillow and grips my forearms with her hands. "I always assumed my legs needed to be spread open in order to have sex. The more you know, huh?" She scrunches her eyes shut and shakes her head again. "What a dumb thing to say."

I move one of her ankles so I can kiss the sole of her foot and flex my hips until I'm so deep inside of her my vision goes hazy for a moment. Fucking ecstasy, every inch of me embraced by her. Slick and warm and tight.

"It's not dumb." Her ignorance is a fucking turn-on and I know I'm a bastard for feeling that way, but fuck it. She's twenty-two, not sixteen, and I'm enjoying the hell out of being the one to introduce her to sex. To watch her squirm and blush. To answer her questions and broaden her horizons. She's so convinced I have some mysterious fetish but I think my fetish is her. Teaching her.

"Well, I am a fairly clever problem-solver," she says with a grin that looks like a secret. Then she tucks her knees tighter to her chest, changing the penetration, and her eyes widen.

"How does this feel?" I ask. "Are you okay?" She's nodding before I'm done asking.

"Good. This is good. More of this, please." She squeezes me and everything gets impossibly tighter and hotter and she's so fucking slick and responsive and perfect as I slide in and out of her. Long slick strokes in and out. She's perfect. Too perfect for me, but I put that out of my mind because I've got enough to fucking think about right now and my only priority at the moment is hearing 'Rhys, Rhys, Rhys' fall from her lips.

That's how she says it when she comes. Every time. 'Oh, oh, oh' followed by 'Rhys, Rhys, Rhys.'

"I want you closer," she says now, her arms reaching for my neck. She drops her knees and spreads her thighs so my hips fit between. Then she pulls me to her, chest to chest. Her perfect little tits are pressed into my chest, our stomachs are pressed flesh to flesh and I hold her head in my hands and kiss her.

"You're nice," she whispers but that can't be right. I'm not nice. I'm paying her for fuck's sake. She's just doing her job. A job she can't possibly need and is either terrible at or great at depending on your viewpoint. I add that to the pile of shit to think about later because Lydia is running her hands over my ass and flexing her hips beneath me so I focus on <u>not</u> improving that average sex time she's so obsessed with and ensuring she's going to feel this all day tomorrow.

After we've gotten to the 'Rhys, Rhys, Rhys' I tell myself I should grab my laptop and send one last email to the London office so I'll have a response by the time I wake up, but Lydia's ass is pressed against my side and her hair is splayed out on my pillow so fuck it. Just fuck it. I'll send the email in the morning.

TWENTY-FOUR

LYDIA

I WONDER IF I look different? If everyone will know I had all the sex this weekend just by looking at me? I peer at myself in Rhys' bathroom mirror and blush. That is the most embarrassing thought ever. And stupid. No one is going to look at me and just know. Besides they were probably doing the same thing all weekend because everyone has sex. Even me.

For example, I will not see Rhys in the office today and imagine what he looks like naked. I will not. If I bump into him in the break room on four I will only think normal thoughts about him. Totally normal, fully clothed thoughts. Because I'm a grown woman and a professional person.

If by chance I happen to pass him in the hallway I will not imagine what he looks like with a towel wrapped around his waist while he stands in front of the mirror shaving. Nope. Absolutely not. In fact, I'm going to stop staring at him right now and try to remove this memory from my brain so it doesn't accidentally pop up later.

"What's wrong?" he asks while I fidget in front of the mirror without looking at him. I just woke up and stumbled in here to pee and found him already out of the shower and—by the looks of it—nearly done shaving. I'd have turned around and used one of the other bathrooms but the toilet in here is in its own private little room, which is the best invention ever because I'm never going to like Rhys a peeing-in-front-of-him amount. I don't think. Unless we get married and have babies and he watches me give birth. Maybe after that it'd be okay to pee in front of him. Firm maybe.

"Nothing." I shrug and grab my toothbrush because I have a toothbrush in Rhys' bathroom. Just a normal Monday morning. I add toothpaste and shove it in my mouth to keep myself from talking. Then I side-eye Rhys again in that towel, except he's done shaving and he's tossed the towel into a basket and is walking naked into his closet and how is a girl not supposed to remember exactly what his naked ass looks like? How? I'm not a magician for crying out loud. I can't just make that visual disappear from my brain. Besides, I don't want to. I want to compose a memo detailing exactly how great his ass looks for every unfortunate female—and any interested male, no hate—who hasn't been lucky enough to be blessed by it firsthand. Which reminds me...

"So, um the office. This," I say, waving a finger between us when he returns fully dressed, knotting a tie around his neck. "The office," I repeat with another wave as I rinse my toothbrush.

"I'll take care of it," he says and then he winks at me and tells me to have a nice lunch and he's gone. Goodness, he starts work early.

Wait.

Lunch?

Oh, God, he's referring to my lunch with Payton.

Referring to hearing Payton ask me for a sex recap during our lunch.

That is... embarrassing.

But he seemed like he was amused so I don't think he minds? Also he worked extra hard at the sex last night so perhaps he reminded me about lunch because he's hoping for a good review.

I take a long shower and dawdle while getting ready because I have the time. I'm up earlier than usual and I've got no commute, which is convenient, even if living in a hotel is a bit weird.

Weird but sorta cool. Unlike not having groceries. That's just weird weird, no matter what Rhys thinks about room service being convenient, I'm not about to call room service every time I want to eat so I'll have to fix the food situation if I'm going to survive a month here. Also he's got a coffeepot and coffee, but no creamer and no organic natural sweetener so what is even the point?

No point at all. Thank goodness for the fancy coffee machine in the break room. That will do for today while I figure out the rest.

Once I'm ready I leave the apartment—or suite; I'm really not sure how to refer to it—and take the private elevator to the fourth floor. Rhys gave me a keycard yesterday that opens his apartment door and accesses the private elevator. He also showed me where the private elevator opens on four so I wouldn't be lost today. I guess he knew he'd be going in to work earlier than me. Which is fine, it's not like I expected him to take the same elevator with me to work. We're not carpooling or anything, just living together and having sex. And getting along well and enjoying each other's company. That's it. I'm absolutely not falling for him. There's only maybe a solid fifty-five percent chance that is happening.

Once I get to work I drop my handbag at my desk. I still brought it to work because it felt weird to leave it upstairs, but it sorta felt unnecessary to bring it when I don't need my car keys or wallet and I already have a spare Chapstick in my desk drawer. This hotel living thing really does come with its own set of complications. Then I head for the break room to fuel up before I start work. Early, like the productive employee I am.

My boss Bethany is productive too because she's already in the break room using the fancy latte machine when I arrive. She smiles and says good morning and comments about how early I am this morning, which I appreciate because verbal acknowledgment is almost as good as a badge.

"Did you have a good weekend?"

I did. I so did.

"Yes, thank you." I mentally pat myself on the back because I'm positive I said that in a normal I-did-not-have-sex tone.

"You look different," she comments idly as she grabs a granola bar from the stash of free snacks arranged in open glass jars on the countertop.

Oh, my God. I have a glow. I have the I-had-the-sex glow. I knew I did. I knew it was going to be super-obvious and now people are going to picture what I look like naked.

"Did you get some sun?"

Or they might just think I got a tan.

"Um, not this weekend, no. But I have gotten some color since moving here. That's probably it." I slide my cup under the coffee dispenser as Bethany removes hers and hit the buttons to select a latte. "What about you?" I ask her as the machine hums and the first drips of coffee sputter into my cup. "Did you do anything fun this weekend?"

"I got a haircut," she answers with a shrug. "Not exactly life-changing. Just a trim," she notes, holding up the ends of a lock of hair.

"Fun," I say for lack of anything better to say. Bethany waits until my drink is ready and then we walk back to our workspaces together. She's got an office at the far end of my row so she leaves me at my cube, telling me to have a good day as she continues down to her office.

I do. I complete an entire list of background checks for a group of food and beverage employees starting this week then dive into preparing a specialized orientation for the spa staff starting tomorrow. I'm having the best day ever until my computer pings with a meeting alert I wasn't aware I had scheduled.

A meeting alert that begins in five minutes.

In Rhys' office.

I'd suspect he was requesting me for some kind of kinky desk sex except that when I click open the meeting icon I see we're not the only meeting attendees. Also he's never been anything but professional towards me at the office—even after I propositioned him in the break room before I knew who he was.

Which, come to think of it, wasn't nearly as bad as hookering myself to him *after* I knew who he was.

So.

That's that.

I'm getting fired.

Bethany is listed as a meeting attendee. As is her boss, Harrison, the vice-president of human resources. And finally, Lawson McCall, head of the legal department at the Windsor—and witness to my sale at Double Diamonds.

I blow out a giant exhale and remind myself about the number of jobs available in my field in Las Vegas. Or I could waitress, like Payton said. I'd probably make more money and have really toned legs from all that running around. This is just so messed up. I thought—I thought I was getting through to Rhys. That he was feeling some of these feelings that I'm feeling, too.

Maybe his fetish is breaking hearts, in which case screw him. I square my shoulders and stand, pushing my desk chair neatly up to my desk because there's no need to be disorderly in times of duress.

I'm wondering which Goodwill I should visit on my way home when Bethany appears at my desk and says she'll walk with me. She's not that much older than me and I wonder if she's ever had to fire someone before. Then I wonder if firing someone is like sex and you always remember your first. And then I wonder if she's not walking with me but escorting me to the meeting and then I stop caring about how hard this might be for her.

We're the last to arrive. I've never been in Rhys' office before. I've never been to any of the executive offices before. I knew where they were, close to my desk in the human resources department, but down a hallway I've never had a need to go down. We pass the private elevator I took to work this morning, located in an alcove just outside the executive hallway, and I give it a sad glance.

Rhys's office is expectedly huge. There's a desk, a seating area with a sofa and coffee table and a conference table positioned in front of the floor-to-ceiling windows with a Las Vegas Boulevard view.

Lawson and Harrison are at the conference table, their postures relaxed. I think I overhear something about a golf score. Par? I don't know, but it sounds like they're talking about golf. Rhys is behind his desk, ignoring both of them, reviewing something or other on a monitor on his desk. He must see us enter the room because he flicks a glance our way with instructions to close the door, then he rises and moves to the conference table, sitting at the head.

Work Rhys isn't that great, actually. He's kinda focused and cold and I decide I'm going to remember him as bar Rhys. Or Del Taco Rhys. Or Goodwill Rhys. The Rhys who watched a home renovation show with me. The Rhys I gave my virginity to and the one I'll never be sorry I went to so much trouble for.

Bethany sits and I take the seat beside her. We're directly across from Lawson and Harrison, the view of the Strip behind their backs.

Then Rhys starts talking.

TWENTY-FIVE

"PER COMPANY POLICY, I need to notify you that Miss Clark and I have recently become involved in a romantic relationship. Due to my position, the board has also been notified."

Oh, holy Jesus.

I turn red, no one says a word and Bethany's eyes widen as she turns her head a fraction to look at me, her expression one of surprise which she quickly tries to mask. Her eyes flicker to Rhys and then back to me and for sure she is thinking about us having sex. Now she knows I don't have a tan glow, I have a sex glow. I bet everyone is thinking about us having sex. Everyone except Rhys because this is still work Rhys and not loves-to-go-down-on-me Rhys.

Oh, God. Now I'm picturing that. Everyone is picturing that.

"We're not dating!" I blurt out. "We're just—"

Rhys raises one eyebrow across the conference table, his expression impassive, save for the tick in his jaw. Right, right. This is our cover and I'm blowing it. He doesn't mean any of this, he's speaking in his work Rhys voice. This is what he meant by taking care of it and I'm blowing it.

"We're just in love is what I meant." Oh, God. That was way over-correcting, but now I've opened my mouth and I can't stop. "He's crazy about me. It's embarrassing really, how into me he is. Really enthusiastically into me." I end on a shrug like I'm just as surprised as anyone by this development. Then I focus all my energy on not slamming my forehead into the table.

Enthusiastically into me sounded like a sex thing, right? No one says someone is enthusiastically into them because of a trip to the Goodwill. A quick look around the table confirms that I might have oversold that because everyone is staring at their laps, except Rhys who is looking at me without blinking, his head tilted to the side and an expression I can't quite identify on his face.

"Any promotion, demotion, salary change or disciplinary action involving Miss Clark will need to be submitted in writing with a copy to Harrison, Lawson and the board," Rhys continues after clearing his throat as if I haven't said a word. "As well as each of her reviews, as they occur."

As they occur? But our relationship will be over before I'm due for a review. Unless he's feeling something too? Unless he finally gets it.

"Obviously these requirements will continue throughout Miss Clark's employment regardless of any future involvement with me."

Oh.

So once we're over I'm still protected from any retaliation in the workplace. That's what this speech is about. He's not telling everyone we're dating. He's telling everyone we're having sex. For now. Sex for now.

While I'm telling everyone we're in love.

Good Lord, he's a lot of work.

Another glance around the table confirms everyone is still staring at their laps except for Lawson. I'm almost certain I just saw him rolling his eyes at Rhys.

There's a moment of dead painful silence and then Rhys excuses us from his office. I don't linger and he doesn't ask me to. Instead, I'm the first to rise, politely push my chair in and bolt from the room.

I'm starting to suspect this grand plan of mine wasn't so grand after all. By the time I get back to my desk I have another meeting, but luckily this one is just a meeting Payton put on my schedule telling me to meet her in the cafeteria, which is perfect timing because I need to decompress. Also I really hope she brought a new badge for me because I could use the confidence boost.

TWENTY-SIX

RHYS

"WHERE'S THE REPORT I asked for on Lydia?" I ask as I walk into Canon's office. I move past his desk without stopping or acknowledging him other than my barked demand and head towards the door that connects his office directly to the security bullpen. There's room for up to twenty people to work in this space, with a glass-encased command center on an elevated platform overlooking them. That's where I head.

I stop in front of the largest monitor. It's mounted on the wall, surrounded by smaller monitors all trained on different areas of the property. Canon strolls in behind me as I'm staring at the controls trying to figure out how to get what I want on the largest monitor.

"Hello to you too, asshole," Canon quips.

"Help me with the cameras." I ignore his dig at my lack of social skills and gesture towards the wall of monitors.

"Finally, you've taken an interest in security." Canon taps at the glass desktop and a control panel appears. "What would you like to see? The casino floor? Loading docks? One of the vaults?" Canon zips images across the large monitor as he talks. I drop into a chair and run a hand over my jaw.

"The employee cafeteria. We've got cameras there, right?"

"The cafeteria," Canon repeats. "Sure. Did you want to know what they're serving for lunch today? Let's see if we can view the menu board from here. What a fantastic use of my time," he adds sarcastically. "I can calculate guest capacity on the casino floor or read the license plate of the armored bank truck arriving, but sure, let's take a look at the cafeteria."

Canon picks up a handheld device and sits, the cafeteria appearing on no fewer than six monitors in front of us from different angles. Lydia's employee ID appears on the main monitor, Canon taps something onto the handheld and a moment later the image flips to a live feed of Lydia. She's sitting at a four-person table in the cafeteria with her friend Payton.

"This is what you are looking for, I assume."

"Shit, how did you find her that fast?"

"I synced the employee IDs with the facial recognition software then created a program that backs the photos into the security feeds. I can tell you where anyone is, what time they arrived on property and what time they left."

"Hmm," I murmur. I'm not that interested in any of this shit but it's because I know Canon has it covered and I don't have to be. "Zoom in."

Canon zooms and the surrounding monitors all redirect to different camera angles of Lydia's table.

"Do we have audio?"

"In the cafeteria?" Canon looks at me like I'm an idiot. "No, we didn't invest in audio on any of the cafeteria security cameras. I can get it installed if stalking Lydia while she's having lunch is going to be your new hobby."

"No, it's fine."

On the monitor ahead of us Payton is holding her hands up, palms facing each other and drawing them apart, then pushing them back together as Lydia blushes and covers her eyes with one hand.

"Payton's really something," Canon says.

"How do you know Payton?"

"Double Diamonds. She was there on Saturday. She's a bit of a handful."

"Did something happen that night?"

"What didn't happen?" Canon exhales with a low whistle. "But that's Vince's problem, thank fuck."

"Right." I wonder if I want him to elaborate on that. I decide I don't. "Do you have my report?"

"I emailed it to you while you were in your meeting."

"What do you know about my meeting?"

"Lawson texted me. He said it was a shit show."

"It was fine."

"He said it's a miracle you've ever gotten laid without paying for it and that Lydia is in love with you and you're fucking it up."

"First of all, I am paying for it. Second of all, Lydia is not in love with me."

"Sure."

On the surveillance monitor Payton has pulled something from her purse and laid it on the table, pushing it towards Lydia.

"Zoom in on that," I tell Canon but he's changed the camera angle to a direct overhead shot before I've finished speaking.

"Blow job," Canon reads the words off the item. It

looks like a seed packet. A cucumber seed packet glued to a piece of felt with 'blow job' written across the top in glitter.

Next Payton slaps down a round circle of denim with 'butt stuff' stamped onto it in black ink and then finally a piece of canvas cut into the shape of a shield with 'SEX' spelled out across the surface. In blue sequins.

"Are these"—Canon sounds a bit incredulously impressed, which is no small feat—"dirty Girl Trooper badges?"

"I think so."

I watch Lydia blush on monitor two and slap her hand over the sex badge and pull it towards her on monitor one. She shakes her head and shoves the 'blow job' and 'butt stuff' badges back towards Payton.

Canon side-eyes the hell out of me.

In the cafeteria Lydia's hand pauses over the blow job badge and she slides it back and forth a little with the tip of her finger. I can see her talking on monitor two and making gestures with her free hand. I imagine she's asking if she can keep the badge or if she has to wait until Wednesday. I've got no idea what she's actually saying of course, but I can picture this pretty clearly. Payton shakes her head and puts two of the three badges back in her bag.

"Shit. Do you have some kind of delayed gratification fetish? Were you that kid who waited until dinner to open your presents from Santa? Did you save your Halloween until Easter?"

"Why does everyone think I have a fetish? I'm just a normal asshole. And Lydia is not a piece of candy."

On the monitor Payton asks Lydia something. Lydia blushes again and runs the sex badge between her fingertips. Then she smiles and makes a swooning gesture.

I swipe open my phone and find the email from Canon. I scan over it—quickly—because there's almost nothing here.

"What am I supposed to do with this?" I ask him.

"I don't know. You're the one who asked for it."

"I thought you'd find me something useful."

"Like what? A secret affiliation to the Russians?"

"I don't know. Credit-card debt or something."

"None. Pays about three hundred a month in student loans. Assuming she's splitting the rent with her roommate, she's paying about eight hundred a month for rent. Add in her car payment, cell phone and utilities and she's got about fifteen hundred a month in disposable income left over each month."

"So she's not desperate."

"Nope."

"Then why? Why the auction?"

"I can't imagine why," Canon deadpans while I stare at the email again.

"She was a Girl Trooper through the twelfth grade?" I look at Canon to see if this is something he slipped in to fuck with me. "Who the hell stays in Girl Troopers that long?"

"Virgins."

Right. So how in the hell did a good girl like her get involved with Vince?

"Are her parents in any financial trouble? Siblings?"

"Only child. Two dads. They own their home, have no debt and have healthy retirement accounts." Canon is ignoring me as he talks, adjusting cameras on the casino floor on one of the smaller monitors. Lydia and Payton are still displayed on the main one.

Payton is talking and Lydia is laughing. I wonder what's amusing her. I wonder how in the hell she slipped into my life and made me feel things for her. Things I don't want and don't have time for, a fact I'm reminded of when my phone rings with yet another call I need to take. I'll have to deal with my goddamned thoughts later. I thank Canon as I stand, phone already pressed to my ear as I exit.

TWENTY-SEVEN

RHYS

I'M SO BUSY I can't think straight. So I don't. I just keep moving through the week. On Monday I don't make it home until after nine. I'd never thought of it as anything but a place to crash in before Lydia took up residence, but she's changed things.

On Wednesday I spilled coffee on the sleeve of my shirt and when I ran up to the apartment to change, it smelled like someone was cooking. Except it was the middle of the day and my kitchen is never used. Besides, I'd just seen Lydia sitting in one of the conference rooms on four, so I knew it wasn't her. Except it was. She'd procured a Crock-Pot from God knows where—no, no, I know exactly where. Based on the pattern of brown flowers the Crock-Pot is older than she is and I know damn well she picked it up at the Goodwill. Half a million dollars doesn't seem to have had any influence on her shopping habits.

Pot roast. She'd made me a pot roast in a Crock-Pot. When I asked her about it after work she said it was no trouble, that she'd ordered groceries from room service and wasn't this easier to have dinner ready whenever we got home? Then she gave me the

225

most unskilled blow job I've had since high school, and I liked it.

I more than liked it.

It was the best, least skilled blow job of my life.

She started by asking if it was okay if she used lube. "It's blueberry," she said, waving the tube in her hand, eyes wide with inquiry. As if the flavor coating my dick made a difference to me. Then she explained that she needed the lube because she didn't want to spit. That the women in the videos she'd watched—for research—had all spit but she thought there must be a better way because while she was really excited about sucking on my cock, she didn't want to spit on it, if that was okay with me.

She actually paused to clarify. "Unless the spitting is the best part? I can spit if you want me to?"

After confirming the lube was new and not picked up during a half-off sale, I gave her my blessing and told her I had no opinion on spit one way or the other. She smiled and flipped the cap open. It wasn't a seductive smile, not in the least. She didn't attempt to gaze at me from under her lashes while licking her lips. She didn't purr like a naughty little kitten. No. She smiled like I'd just held open a door for her and wiggled her fingers in excited anticipation as if she wasn't sure where to start. Then she flipped open the cap and squeezed twice the needed amount into her palm and wrapped her hand around my dick, her nose wrinkling when she realized the overuse of lube had made it way messier than she'd anticipated.

I almost blew my load right there.

"Oh," she murmured. "Okay, one second. I can fix this." Then she stood, returning with a hand towel from the bathroom. Once she wiped off her hand she dropped to her knees again, this time an earnest look on her face as she looked up at me, kneeling between my spread thighs. "Ready?" she asked me, wrapping her palm around me again, and, finding the lubrication more to her liking, she slid her hand down to the base and back to the tip before leaning forward and wrapping her lips around the head, a hint of tongue swiping across the slit.

That's when a strand of her hair got stuck in the lube.

She stopped again, attempting to pull it free before I took over for her and held it off her face in a fisted ponytail, refraining from setting the pace for her. She licked me, root to tip, with her tongue flat on the underside of my cock. She managed three inches, if that, sucking and swirling her tongue. Then she sat back and said, "Okay, now choke me with it." She smiled, as if asking me to choke her with my cock was a favor to her instead of me.

I told her no and another conversation about why not and when took place. I don't think a month is going to be long enough to teach her how to choke on my cock. I don't think a month is going to be long enough, period.

Then she asked if she could swallow—of course she asked—and afterwards we ate pot roast in front of the television while watching a show about house flippers.

Home-cooked pot roast. From a Crock-Pot.

It seems she obtained some historical Tupperware to match the Crock-Pot, because she filled a container with leftovers and put it in my fridge. A fridge now containing coffee creamer and hummus, grapes, cheese and I don't know what the hell else.

On Sunday I was about to grab something from my home office when I passed the guest bedroom and did a double-take. I hadn't realized she'd put anything in this room, but she had. She'd set up a sewing machine on the desk. The machine looked relatively new, meaning sometime from the past decade, so I guessed it wasn't a recent Goodwill find but something she'd run back to grab from her apartment. There were stacks of cut-up bed sheets on top of the dresser and spools of elastic and ribbon. Folded over the back of the armchair were two completed pairs of pajama pants. From deducing the obvious, they were made out of sheets.

She makes her own pajamas out of old sheets.

I'm not sure if I hired a hooker or a housewife.

I am sure I'm a dick. I made her move in and left her alone every night this week. I only managed to eat dinner with her twice. The remaining nights I got home late, swept in and made love—fucked her. I fucked her and then slept, slipping out in the morning to the gym while she was still asleep. Joining her in the shower some mornings, at my desk downstairs before she's awake on others.

Yet staring at this hobby of hers that I knew nothing about, I feel like an ass. But she makes me want to try. Try to be different. Try to be better. Try to slow down and give a shit about what's real and what matters. And I think she's real.

And she makes me laugh. During the commercial break of one of her house-hunting shows an advertisement came on for washing machines, touting their deep fill cycles. She ran her hand up my thigh and said, "I like it when you fill me deep, Rhys."

I laughed, not realizing it was an attempt at seduction, not a joke. She blinked, that slightly hurt look she gets when she thinks she's being rejected crossing her face. So I kissed her and used washing-machine analogies to dirty-talk her until she was smiling again.

Jesus Christ. I think I might love her.

TWENTY-EIGHT

LYDIA

RHYS WORKS A LOT but I get this weird sense he's trying to make time for me. As if he's trying to impress me, which I think means he likes me. Maybe even in a more-than-thirty-days kind of way. Not to sound conceited or without humility, but I thought he might. I thought if he just gave me a chance he might like me in a several-months kind of way instead of a two-day-shipping kind of way.

That was the plan after all.

Sorta the plan.

Falling in love with him was not the plan. And it's also against the rules. Just sex, he said. That's the rule, he said.

He told me there was no happily-ever-after for us but I didn't listen and now there's a solid sixty percent chance that I'm in love with him. Which is going to be really problematic if he decides that thirty days of me is more than enough for him. Problematic for me, anyway. But I've not lost hope, because I've still got two weeks left. The official grand opening of the Windsor is tonight and it also marks the halfway point in our... arrangement.

But I have reason to hope because, for example,

last Sunday he woke me up with an iced java coffee from Del Taco and two egg and cheese burritos. In bed. He brought me Del Taco in bed. So I think he really likes me, because that's wooing. You don't take the elevator to the parking garage, get in your car, drive down the street, wait in the drive-thru, <u>and</u> remember a girl's breakfast order unless you feel something. Right?

Also, for another example, we keep having sex for way longer than seven to thirteen minutes. Although one morning we did have a quickie in the shower, but even that took at least ten minutes. Since the internet turned out to be an oddly unreliable source of information on this topic, I asked Payton about it. She explained to me that most guys can get off in approximately three minutes if they're not concerned about the woman's pleasure, so I think it stands to reason that Rhys is keenly concerned with my pleasure.

Last Sunday after he brought me breakfast in bed he demonstrated his keenness. Multiple times. Then we showered together and went to Goodwill. Yes, Goodwill! Two weekends in a row. If that's not wooing, I don't know what is. Sure, some girls might prefer a fancy dinner but I am not those girls. And I didn't even ask him to take me! It was his idea. After our shower he told me to get dressed so we could run to the store. I thought maybe he wanted to go the grocery store because he'd seemed really perplexed when I'd told him I was ordering groceries from room service, but he took me to Goodwill. And—and! It was a different one than we'd gone to the weekend prior. Meaning he had to have used the store finder on their website. Which means—honestly it means scratch the sixty percent chance. I am seventy-five percent confirmed in love with him.

After our trip to the Goodwill (I scored a set of embroidered vintage sheets) we went to the Forum Shops at Caesars. Which confirmed that driving to the Goodwill on Sahara was totally out of the way and was further proof that Rhys may, in fact, be enthusiastically into me. I found a dress to wear to the grand opening and then we had a late lunch at the Palm. Just like a real date. He even talked to me the entire time without looking at his phone once. He asked how long I've been sewing and didn't laugh at me when I explained about the sheet pajamas.

It's almost like Rhys has forgotten that he paid me to be here. For my part I've done my best to pretend I forgot how I got here.

Vince, however, has not forgotten.

Not even close to forgotten.

In fact, he's been pretty busy.

And helpful since we've been collaborating on another... idea. I've been putting him off because I'm not ready to make any decisions about what's next because I'm in a bubble right now. I'm happy in the bubble and I don't want the bubble punctured by anything. So truthfully, I've been ignoring Vince a little.

Mostly because he keeps asking me weird things like have I talked to Payton today, which I don't understand because I've already explained to him that I'm not being kept captive and I talk to Payton whenever I want to. It's nice of him to be concerned about me though, and he has done me an awfully big favor so I should be more polite. Ignoring someone is quite rude and un-Trooper-like behavior. I feel chastised just thinking of it.

TWENTY-NINE

LYDIA

THE GRAND OPENING is a bit nerve-racking because I have to be Rhys' girlfriend in public. Sure, the last two weeks at work might be considered public but we don't interact in the office. Like ever. I see him in passing, but I keep my swooning tucked inside where it belongs. But tonight at the grand opening everyone will see us together and picture us naked. Right? Or maybe that's just me. Maybe I'm the only one who does that.

Anyway.

This morning was the official ribbon-cutting. The mayor of Las Vegas was on hand to assist with the literal ribbon-cutting. A giant pair of scissors was used and I wondered where they came from and if every casino in Las Vegas kept their own pair on hand or if there was just one pair that was passed around the city for special events. I also wondered where giant scissors were purchased because I've never seen a pair at the Goodwill and if everyone in Vegas had their own you'd think sooner or later there'd be an excess of them, what with all the grand openings and special events that occur here on a regular basis.

I decided I'll take a closer look during my next shop.

I met Rhys' parents and his grandmother at dinner last night. He introduced me as his girlfriend, which of course he would. It's not like he's going to introduce me to his mother as an escort. But it was hard because his mother loved me so I felt massive amounts of deep-seated Trooper guilt for deceiving her. But maybe it doesn't count as actual deceit since I am in fact eighty percent in love with her son. This seems like a gray area.

She enthusiastically gushed over me though, for the record.

She also said she'd love to have us to Connecticut for Christmas. I had no idea what I was supposed to say to that because of course I *wanted* to go to Connecticut for Christmas but I had no idea if I'd still be with Rhys by Christmas because Christmas is way past the thirty-day bubble.

"Are you ready?" Rhys exits his walk-in closet in the midst of knotting his second tie of the day. After the ribbon-cutting, which I attended, and a press tour, which I did not, we both came back to the apartment to change for the evening activities. We did the shower sex again too. I did it on one foot because Rhys pinned me to the wall with one of my legs raised and propped over his arm. I need to talk to Payton because I feel as though that maneuver might be worthy of its own badge.

"Can you zip me?" I ask, turning my back to him. I only managed to get the zipper halfway up without assistance.

"I'd rather unzip you," he murmurs into my ear, a single finger trailing the path of the zipper against my skin. "But you already look just-fucked enough for my liking," he adds, pulling the zipper smoothly closed.

I look at us in the reflection of the mirror, a bit alarmed. I knew I was right about that. Everyone is going to be thinking about us having sex. It's inevitable. And looking at him, I can't blame them. It was the first thing I imagined upon seeing him for the first time too.

"Do I really look like I just had sex? How can you tell?" I lean closer to the mirror and examine my eyes. "Obviously I get that everyone would assume I'm having sex with you every chance that I get, but how can they tell if it was an hour ago or last night?"

Rhys pauses in the act of slipping a cufflink into his shirtsleeve and stares at me. He narrows his eyes slightly, in that way he does when he's unsure if I'm serious or not.

"Let's table that thought for now," he says, but I continue to stare at myself in the mirror, wrinkling my nose and turning my head from side to side, trying to figure out what my tell is so I can stop emitting the just-had-sex beacon.

"Don't worry about it," Rhys says after fastening the second cufflink. "I was joking. I'll tell everyone you're still a virgin."

"As if I went through this much trouble not to have sex with you," I scoff.

"What does that mean?" Rhys is doing the narrowed eyes thing again.

"Um..." Shoot. "Let's table that thought too." I slip my feet into my heels and grab my clutch. "We're going to be late."

"It's an all-night event. We can't technically be late."

Uh-huh.

"Do you like my clutch?" I hold up the bag for viewing. "I found it at Goodwill. It's cute, right? Do you want me to carry your gum or anything?" It's a black clutch with a sequined pair of swans on the front.

"I don't chew gum. Listen, I know I've been busy, but we can't continue on like this. We need to talk."

Wait, what?

"Yes, yes, we can continue on like this. For two more weeks we can continue on like this. Exactly like this."

"Exactly like this?" His jaw ticks when he says it.

"Yes!" Why in the heck is he trying to rob me of my last two weeks with him? That's half my allotted time! And I know he likes me, I know he does. And he likes me more than a like amount. He just needs to come to terms with it or something.

Rhys' phone rings and when he glances at the screen to silence it I slide past him out of the bathroom and nearly sprint for the front door.

"Lydia." He's right behind me but I keep moving. "Hold on."

I ignore him and swing the door open, nearly bumping right into Canon.

"Hey!" I plaster a huge smile on my face, which isn't hard because I am so glad for the interruption.

"I was about to knock," Canon says with a hint of sarcasm, but it appears to be directed at Rhys not me so I keep on smiling and step into the hallway.

The executive elevator doesn't connect directly to the casino floor, so we have to take it to the parking garage level and then switch to a different elevator bank to reach the guest areas. Rhys is silent. I'm silent. Canon is oblivious, checking his cell phone, until he notices the silence. He looks up, his thumb moving across the screen, and glances between us.

"Everything okay?"

"Of course," I reply.

"Is it?" Rhys says at the same time.

Canon's eyes bounce between us again and he mutters, "Okay then," as the elevator doors open and we're thrust into a crowd of people. Canon leads the way as Rhys takes my hand and my heart skips a beat at the gesture. He keeps me held close to him but I don't know if it's because of the crowd or because of appearances or because he simply wants me close.

I hope it's because he wants me close.

The next hour is a dizzying hail of introductions and socializing. Of smiling and hand-shaking and pretending. I'm introduced to Rhys' British cousin Jennings. He's also the CEO of the parent company that owns the Windsor, so I suppose that makes him my boss' boss' boss' boss. Luckily he has no memory of me whatsoever, since he was there that night I first met Rhys at the bar. He was drunk and denouncing love at the time, so I don't expect he'd remember. It appears he's sorted out his love issues because I'm introduced to his fiancée Violet. She's American, so I ask how she met Jennings when we're left on our own, Rhys and Jennings having been pulled off to greet some bigwig or another.

"Well, I was impersonating my identical twin sister. Who was employed with the company in the tour division."

"Oh."

"Jennings was on vacation with his nan and ended up on my tour. Well, my sister's tour."

"Uh huh."

"Then it became this *Undercover Boss* sort of

thing," she says, waving her free hand around. The other is holding a wine glass. "Because he never told me he owned the company."

"Right." I wonder if this is a real story or some kind of weird initiation? She doesn't appear to be in the least drunk, so it can't be that.

"But we worked it out," she finishes with a big smile. "So how did you and Rhys meet?"

"Um, in a bar." *The normal way,* I think to myself. Of course the whole virgin auction thing doesn't give me a whole lot of room to be a Judgey McJudgeypants. Then something else occurs to me. "Has Rhys heard this story?" Maybe he won't think what I did was so weird in comparison. It's not like I've impersonated anyone.

"Oh, I'm sure. They're very close. Hey, are those the LK Bennett Sledge pumps?"

"Um." I look down at my feet and then back to Violet. "I think so? I got them at LK Bennett when I bought the dress. I'm not sure which style they are."

"They're Princess Kate's favorite shoe," she tells me.

"Oh. Okay."

"Sorry, I'm a bit of an Anglophile."

"I guess having a British fiancé really works for you then, huh?"

"It does. It so does. Plus I get to listen to him speak in that sexy British accent whenever I want. Sometimes I ask him questions just to hear him speak. Last week I asked him to explain the history of the European Union to me. He went on for half an hour before he realized I just wanted to listen to him use words like 'referendum' and 'organization.'"

I can't fault her logic.

Jennings comes back to retrieve Violet just as

Payton slips up beside me, looking over her shoulder.

"Hey!" I pull her into a quick hug. "It's good to see you. Now tell me who you're avoiding."

"Vince."

"He's here?"

"He's freaking everywhere."

Huh.

"I think he's friends with Canon," I mention. "Canon probably invited him to the VIP event."

"Sure," she says quickly. Too quickly. "That's probably why he's here."

A waiter pauses in front of us with a tray of hors d'oeuvres. I shake my head no as Payton grabs some kind of mini puff pastry and shoves it into her mouth. Shoving food into her mouth is one of her favorite diversionary tactics. She must be wearing some of that magical lipstick that stays on for hours, because she manages to down it with nary a smudge.

"Are you in some sort of trouble?"

"Of course not." She waves her hand while shaking her head at the same time, but she won't look at me. "I'm taking care of it."

"Taking care of what?" I narrow my eyes in suspicion. Come to think of it, she's been acting a little bit shady ever since the auction. It was easy to miss until now because I've been living with Rhys and distracted with all the sexing stuff, but something is off.

"The thing. I'm going to fix it. It's just turning out to be a bit more complicated than one would think. And I didn't realize he'd be here tonight. I thought work was a safe zone but here he is." She's holding a glass of champagne and she takes a gulp and does another scan of the room then twists the glass in her fingers. Her blonde hair is pulled demurely into a updo and she's wearing a pale blush dress with three-quarter sleeves and a modest—for her—mid-thigh hemline. It makes her look like an innocent angel but that is a lie.

"What thing, Payton? What's going on?"

"Nothing. I'll tell you later," she adds when I give her a look implying I'm not buying anything she's selling. She looks past me and her eyes widen. "Listen, I've got to go. Love you! We'll talk later." She starts to edge past me without waiting for a reply but she's trapped between a waiter weighted down with a serving tray filled with champagne glasses and an actress taking a selfie with I don't know who. She spins, looking for another avenue of escape, when Vince stops directly in front of us.

He's dressed in a black suit with a perfectly pressed white shirt and he looks like a million dollars. More tall, dark and Italian than pseudo-pimp and confirmed strip club owner. He also looks pissed.

At Payton.

That much is clear because he's not looking at me, he's looking at her. Payton for her part is still attempting to find a pocket of space to slink away in.

"Mrs. Rossi," he says. "Stop. Right. There."

Oh. Maybe he's not looking at Payton. Rossi, that's his last name. I didn't realize he was married. I turn my head to get a peek at his wife but no one is there. The actress and selfie-taker are gone. It's just Payton and the waiter and the waiter is already moving away. Payton snags a fresh glass of champagne from his tray at the last second and downs it in one long continuous gulp.

I look from Vince to Payton and back again.

Vince is still staring at Payton.

Payton glances at me and shrugs before her eyes dart over to Vince and then away.

"You married him?" I almost shriek it. In fact, I think I did shriek but the casino floor is loud enough to mask my outburst.

"Freaking Las Vegas, am I right?" Payton holds her free hand palm up and raises her eyebrows as if to say the city of Las Vegas is entirely responsible for her marital status. As if it's the same thing as complaining about the traffic on Las Vegas Boulevard or the temperature in summer.

She's entirely too nonchalant.

"When?" I demand. "When did this happen? How did this happen? You only met him two weeks ago! Payton! And"—I point my finger at her then stab it into my chest—"and you didn't even invite me?"

"I would have," Payton responds slowly as if I'm being irrational, "if I'd known it was happening. I absolutely would have invited you. You'd have made a much better maid of honor than Canon, that's for sure. My hair was a mess and he didn't even tell me. The wedding photos are horrible."

"There are photos?"

"Yeah. I think they came with the package. Did they come with the package, Vince?" She turns to him as if she wasn't just in the midst of trying to hide from him and as if he's not still in the midst of killing her with his eyes. "Pretty sure," she says again. "But good point. Maybe Canon took some with his phone that are better than the professional ones."

"That clearly wasn't my point."

"Oh."

"When did this happen?"

"Um, sometime after the auction but before the

next morning." She waves her hand in an arc. "Somewhere in there. Things got"—she pauses—"a little crazy. I don't want to beat a dead horse about you missing it, but that night was a real good time."

I glance between her and Vince again. Confused.

"So why are you avoiding Vince now?" I question. "Vince, also known as your husband."

"Calm down. Everyone knows what happens in Vegas isn't legally binding."

"That's not a thing that is true," I reply as Vince exhales loudly and closes the distance between himself and Payton, placing his hand on her lower back in a pretty obvious attempt to keep her from escaping.

"Enough. We need to talk," Vince tells her.

"Ugh. Talking is the worst," Payton groans, dragging out the word 'ugh' and dropping her head back in exasperation. She stomps one heeled foot in added protest.

For once, I have to agree with Payton. Also, I'm wondering if they had sex yet.

THIRTY

RHYS

LYDIA IS TALKING TO Vince and she's upset. Agitated. While I'm trapped talking to the governor of Nevada, a board member from the UK and a high-roller from Hollywood whose name I can't remember even though we were introduced not five minutes ago. Because I'm distracted. The one thing I wanted to avoid during this opening was distractions and I've ended up with the biggest distraction of my life.

I'm irritated for allowing this to happen. Allowing Lydia to wiggle into my life and disrupt everything.

I'm aggravated that I can't hear what they're talking about. That I don't know why she's upset or what's causing her eyes to widen and her lips to pout.

Fucking Vince. I'm putting an end to this tonight. Why do I even associate with people like this? What am I doing? The arrangement with Lydia can't continue like this. Not for another day.

Except it will have to, because Vince disappears shortly after I spot him talking to Lydia. And I never get a chance to speak to Lydia about what's upset her because we're torn in different directions for the rest of the evening, or surrounded by swarms of people.

Everyone loves her. I get it, I do, but I don't want to share. I want her all to myself like the selfish prick I am. I want to drag her upstairs and find out what Vince wanted, then make love to her until she does the 'oh, oh, oh' and the 'Rhys, Rhys, Rhys.'

But that does not happen. When we're finally headed upstairs for the night I get pulled away to speak with the president of a major liquor company, a woman who's flown in from France to attend the grand opening, so talk I must. Lydia heads upstairs without me and she's sound asleep by the time I join her thirty minutes later.

Sunday morning I rise to find that Lydia is up before me, which never happens. "We need to talk," I tell her the moment I walk into the living room. I've just stepped out of the shower, a towel still wrapped around my waist. It smells like a bakery in here and Lydia is slicing bananas at the kitchen island. She's awake and dressed and somehow I'm already feeling three steps behind on this day. I checked my messages before I went into the shower so I know I haven't overslept. I also know I've got no fewer than a dozen voicemails that require an answer and Jennings wants to meet at ten to go over the forecasting reports for the next quarter.

And it's Sunday. And I'm tired as fuck. And all I want to do is eat breakfast on the couch with Lydia and watch whatever home show is on at nine in the morning.

"What's going on with you and Vince?"

"What?" Lydia looks up at me in confusion. "Oh, that. Crazy stuff. I made French toast casserole with Nutella and caramelized bananas. In the Crock-Pot, see how handy it is? I just have to sauté these bananas for the top and it's ready."

The Crock-Pot. That'd be why it smells like someone fucking cares in here.

"How much more do you need?"

"What?"

"I want you to stay. So how much more do you need? I'll talk to Vince and take care of it."

She slow-blinks at me for several seconds as my phone pings with another goddamned message.

"I've got a lot of calls to make, but I want to take care of this. Today. So what's your price?"

Lydia turns away and places a frying pan I didn't know I owned on the stove. Scratch that, I'm sure I don't own a frying pan. She must have procured it from somewhere. I wonder if she ordered it from room service with the groceries? I wonder if I'll ever stop finding her so endlessly fascinating.

Lydia is fiddling at the stove, ignoring me, so I return to the bedroom to grab my phone, tapping out a text as I return to the kitchen.

"Say something to me, Rhys. Say something to me that is not what you just said."

"I'm not sure what you want me to say." I want to know what the fuck she was talking to Vince about last night. I want to know how she feels about me. I want to resolve all this uncertainty. My phone pings again and I glance at it before sending the call to voicemail.

"Do you know what, Rhys? I think you're so afraid of anything real that you hide behind work and strip clubs and general stupidity."

What? Okay. I blow out a breath. Okay, I might have this all wrong. "Wait, so—"

"No, I don't want to wait. I'm not much of a waiter, Rhys. In case you haven't noticed. I'm a doer and I've done everything. You're a decade older than me. You're the one with all the experience and confidence and life skills and yet I'm the one doing everything. Every. Freaking. Thing." She says that last bit slowly, like she's punctuating the words.

"Okay. Let's slow down here. If this is about breakfast we can always order from room service."

"Oh, my God." She snaps the stove off and puts down a wooden spoon. I didn't know I owned one of those either. "Yeah, Rhys. This is about who makes breakfast. Listen to yourself. You're thirty-four years old. Wake up. Pay attention to what's going on in your life for half a second. How about that?"

"I am," I snap back. "I paid attention to your little pow-wow with Vince last night. Which is why I—"

"You think I'm having secret meetings with Vince, Rhys?" she interrupts again. "In the middle of the grand opening in front of everyone? Yes. Absolutely. I was lining up my next assignment before I came upstairs to Google Crock-Pot recipes for breakfast."

"I don't want you with anyone else, Lydia."

"But you don't quite want me yourself, do you? Not for real." She shakes her head and presses her lips together before taking a deep breath. "Ask me how this feels, Rhys."

It feels suspiciously like I've taken a wrong turn this morning.

"Never mind. I'll tell you. It feels like... like being empty." She shrugs when she says it but it's a sad shrug, maybe even on the side of belligerent. "It feels like getting to an amusement park and finding out they're filled to capacity and you can't get in. It feels like someone just told me Santa isn't real before I was ready. It feels like it's raining inside my heart."

I notice a moment too late that she's grabbed her handbag and looped the strap over her head as she walks to the door.

"Just for the record, I was ninety-three percent in love with you. I deducted five percent for being financially irresponsible because you could have had me for free if you weren't so afraid of your stupid feelings. And two percent for being an idiot. I'm probably double-counting the idiot percents with the money percents but you know what, I don't care."

"Lydia, wait." I attempt to catch the door with my hand, to keep her from opening it, which is just shitty and she rewards me with a look that says as much. And then she's gone.

Fuck. What the hell just happened?

THIRTY-ONE

RHYS

I FUCKED THAT UP. I fucked that up and I've got no idea where she went. I called Canon as I was getting dressed, one hand on the phone and one yanking a shirt over my head, and asked him to track her from the door of my suite, hoping that she was somewhere in the hotel. Knowing she wouldn't be.

She wasn't. She took the elevator to the parking garage, got in her car and exited the property just under two minutes later. And she's not going to answer if I call because her phone is sitting on the nightstand next to my bed, charging.

Fuck.

She probably wouldn't have answered anyway, but I hate that she's without her phone. What if her car breaks down or she runs out of gas or she wants to call anyone who isn't me?

I don't even know who her friends are, outside of Payton, or if she's made friends yet since moving to Vegas. I tell Canon to get hold of Payton with instructions to call me if Lydia goes back to her apartment. Then I open the Goodwill app on my phone as I get into my car. Would she go to the one between the Windsor and her apartment? I don't think her car has GPS, so she won't be able to find locations she hasn't been to yet, but that doesn't eliminate a single store because she's probably been to every fucking one of them.

Why are there so many goddamned Goodwill stores in Greater Las Vegas? I slide into my car and head to the one on Tropicana. It's the first one we went to together, two weeks ago, and it's between my place and hers. The parking lot is too crowded to do a quick search for her car so I run in. She's not there. Of course she's not there, because why should this be easy? I don't deserve for this to be easy. I call Canon and ask if he can hack into the city surveillance cameras to track her from the time she left the parking garage.

He laughs at me and hangs up.

I call him back and tell him to cover for me because I'm taking the day off. Because Lydia is right about everything. Because I haven't been paying attention to my own life and now the best part of it is gone. I sling the phone into the passenger seat as I get back in my car and wrestle with whether she'd have gone to the location on Maryland, or the one on Sahara that I took her to last week. Or would she have headed to one of the half-dozen locations in Henderson, closer to her apartment? Jesus. I decide to give the one on Maryland a shot. It's closer to the hotel than the one on Tropicana, so maybe she went to that one first. Or maybe I'm going to spend the day chasing her from one donation center to the next.

I'll chase her as long as I need to. As long as she'll let me.

She's not at the Maryland location. She's not at her apartment. And she's not been back to the hotel.

It's time to pay Vince a visit.

THIRTY-TWO

RHYS

"WHERE IS LYDIA?"

I've located Vince in his office at Double Diamonds and I've skipped formalities. I'm so far past the mood for polite behavior with this asshole.

"I sent her to look at some property," Vince replies, unbothered by my arrival or attitude. He's not even looking at me, too busy on his laptop to bother. He's probably tallying the night's receipts, or placing an order for pole sanitizer, fucking dirtbag. "Did you want her back?"

I tell myself that killing him will only delay getting to Lydia. "Yes, I want her back, asshole. What hold do you have over her, Vince? How much does she owe you? Name your price so we can be done with this charade."

"Another million would change things," he says slowly, leaning back in his chair as he examines me with interest.

"Fine. I'll wire it to you today and then you're done with her. Now tell me where I can find her."

"You're an idiot." He leans forward in his chair again and pins me with a stare. "And never speaking to Lydia again is going to be problematic for me."

"Why is that?"

"I'm married to her best friend, for starters."

I stare at him, waiting for the words to make sense. "You married Payton?" I feel like I'm missing something. I drop into the chair across from Vince and take the edge off my glare. Just a bit. I'm not ready to be wrong about Vince yet. Besides, he's still an asshole regardless.

"Yes. I married Payton, God help me. As far as Lydia is concerned, you are the only person who can't see straight through her if you haven't figured this out by now."

"What's that supposed to mean?"

"She's transparent as fuck. You don't even know how lucky you are. I wish Payton was so transparent. I have no idea what the fuck she's thinking or where she even is most of the time."

"What are you saying exactly?"

"That auction was all for you. Prostitution isn't even legal in Clark County, Rhys. The entire thing was a setup. Do you think I'm running half a million through my books for the sale of a virgin? This is a gentleman's club, not a brothel, you dumb fuck."

"Yeah, like there's no prostitution happening in Las Vegas," I counter. "We both know that's not the case."

"Sure enough. But not through me. I'm running a legitimate business here."

Fuck my life. We stare at each other across his desk and I know he's telling me the truth, I'm almost certain of it. But, fuck. Have I really paid this little attention?

"What about that guy I was bidding against? Stan?"

"Stan is my maintenance man and that suit cost

me a grand. I'm sending you the bill for that, by the way."

"There was an email," I counter. "A newsletter."

"A newsletter," he repeats back to me like I'm an idiot. "Sure, I sell sex through a newsletter, Rhys. I gain subscribers through newsletter swaps with all the other brothels in the state," he deadpans and yeah, I see it now. I'm an idiot. "We get together at Starbucks and brainstorm ways to cross-promote," he continues. "You've found us out. Good job."

"I get it. The newsletter was fake," I fill in but it's unnecessary because Vince isn't listening to me anyway.

"That was Canon's idea. I told him it was too stupid to be believable but he said—"

"Yeah, I'm an idiot. I got it," I interrupt, anxious to get to the part where I find Lydia and fix this. I wave my hand for him to continue.

"He said you were really distracted," Vince continues. "And that the visual would help get you here."

Canon has always loved a visual.

"Wait. How did Canon get involved in this? I still don't understand where this entire plot came from in the first place."

"Lydia," Vince replies like I'm especially slow. "It was all Lydia's idea. From what she told me, you two had a thing in a bar but she thought you had a paying-for-it fetish because you couldn't seal the deal with her."

Vince could not be any less impressed with me right now. He just held up two fingers and bent them in the universal air quote gesture while he said 'paying-for-it fetish.'

"I don't—"

"I don't want to know," he interrupts with a shake of his head. "I called Canon to find out if anything she was saying was real or if he needed me to call the police to report that you had a nutcase following you around. Canon confirmed that the two of you did have a thing." He air-quotes again here when he says 'a thing' as if it's ridiculous to him. "And he was quite taken with Lydia's grand plan to seduce you into admitting you were interested in her by staging an auction. I was feeling especially charitable that day, as it were, so we collaborated on how best to get you here."

I make a mental note to cut Canon's staff. He really does have too much time on his hands.

"So what was the money for? Why the hell did you goad me into half a million if all of this is fake?" I ask, but my mind is racing with how epically I've blown this with Lydia.

"I'm not a stranger to charitable donations, Rhys. Getting you to fund a charitable cause was the least you could do to reimburse me for my time."

"You're a real dick, you know that?"

Vince shrugs. "It was for a good cause."

"The cause being?" I question. "Gold-leaf nipple pasties for everyone?"

"Lydia didn't want the money," Vince replies, ignoring my dig as he drags a finger across the mousepad on his laptop. "I was gouging you for my own entertainment. And the cause, of course," he adds, flashing a sardonic grin at me.

"Right. The cause. Which is?"

"New campground," Vince retorts, flipping his laptop around to face me. "For the Girl Troopers of Greater Las Vegas. Found a great property out at Red Rock, but the property is lacking a suitable cabin. There's one there but it was abandoned a decade ago and the agent said it's uninhabitable. Plus you know how hot it gets here," he says, brow rising in meaning. "A pool would be a nice addition. For the campers."

"That's what you need a million for?"

"Yeah. Assuming Lydia likes the property. I'll get the land into escrow, then hire a general contractor to level the existing cabin and build something up to code. Add in a pool, maybe a tennis court. Then we'll donate it to the Girl Troopers."

"She'll want to renovate." I sigh. "She'll want to save whatever dilapidated structure is still standing with some romantic vision of its historic charm. Even if it's a pile of shit from the 1980's. We'll need to hire someone who can renovate or use whatever's left of it to build a porch swing or some shit like that. It'll make her happy."

"Fine with me." He shrugs. He pulls a Post-It from his desk drawer and scribbles down the campsite address before passing it over to me. "Are we done here? I'll send you a receipt for your charitable donation. Don't let the door hit you on the way out and you might still catch her there."

"Thank you, Vince."

"She's too good for you."

"I know. I want her anyway." If it's not too late. It can't be too late because I can't go back to a life without Lydia in it.

THIRTY-THREE

RHYS

RED ROCK IS JUST outside of Vegas and per the GPS on my car I should be at this campsite Vince is sending me to in just over half an hour. Which means I've got half an hour to sit in my car and think about what an asshole I am. It's ten straight miles down Charleston until the road curves and I start winding my way towards the campground.

It takes another ten minutes and a nearly missed turn to reach my destination and I'm relieved to see two cars parked outside an old cabin that should surely be condemned. I park beside Lydia's car and scan the area, unsure if they're inside or walking the property. There's no door on the cabin, or much of a roof really. I don't see anyone so I head for the door. Or the doorway, as it were.

I hear her voice as soon as I cross the threshold. She's standing with the real-estate agent facing a window in the side of the cabin, the glass long gone. There's a view of Red Rock Canyon in the background but it doesn't hold a candle to a glimpse of Lydia.

"I picked a bad swan," she's telling the woman. "I picked a bad swan and I mated with him and now

I'm stuck with him because I'm ninety-three percent in love with him even though he's an idiot." She shakes her head and then stops abruptly, leaning towards the real-estate agent. "Not the pregnant kind of mating, just the fun kind. Can I say that? I was a Trooper for thirteen years, you know. I earned all the health badges so I know how reproductive mating works and I've covered my bases. I'm probably going to earn a 'didn't get knocked up by accident' badge."

"Um..." The agent stalls, tilting her head to the side, clearly not sure how to respond to anything that just came out of Lydia's mouth. Then she spots me and relief covers her face. "Well, look at that. Looks like your swan came for you."

Lydia whirls and her eyes flash in surprise. A look of confusion follows.

"Rhys." She sighs it a little when she says it, and it sounds like a question.

"I'll leave you two." The real-estate agent smiles and with a glance between us turns to leave. Her heels snap across the floor until she reaches the porch, Lydia and I silent until she's gone. Then I close the distance between us, walking slowly towards her while taking in the interior of the cabin.

"Nice place," I say by way of easing in.

"Yeah." She nods. "Yeah, it is. It's got a lot of potential." She lifts her chin a fraction. "With the right vision it could be really special."

"I'm sorry." She blinks rapidly and takes a breath but I continue before she can say anything. "I'm sorry for everything. Except for that first kiss in the bar. That was the best decision I've ever made. I'm sorry for everything that came after."

"You're sorry?" She blinks again "Sorry in a 'you

wish it didn't happen' kind of way?"

"God, no." I shake my head. "Sorry in an 'I'm in love with you' way. In an 'I'm hoping I haven't fucked it up too badly' kind of way. In an 'I'm hoping you'll give me another chance' kind of way."

"Oh."

"I'm sorry for giving you such mixed signals. I'm sorry for walking out on you at the bar and I'm sorry I put you in a position to resort to such a completely insane plan to get my attention."

"I'm sorry too. My timing wasn't great. I should have waited until after the grand opening, but I was afraid you'd fall in love with a real hooker instead of me."

"Not possible." I shake my head.

"Sure it is. Anything is possible."

"You're the only woman for me, Lydia. I don't know what I can offer you," I say softly, tucking a strand of hair behind her ear and bringing her hand to my lips. "But I'm in love with you and I want to try."

"What are you doing?" She looks alarmed and takes a step back, her hand dropping from mine. "Are you proposing to me right now?"

"I wasn't, actually. But I can. I'll marry you today if that's what it takes."

"No!"

"Okay, wow. That was a pretty spirited no. So you don't want to marry me?"

"We met less than two months ago, Rhys. I want to be courted. Wooed. Pursued. Solicited in a romantic fashion. At someplace other than Del Taco. No, that's a lie. Del Taco is fine, actually."

"You want to be wooed with value-menu iced coffee?"

"It's really good, Rhys. No matter what you say."

"Fair enough."

"Here's a spoiler, Rhys: I will marry you. Someday. But this"—she gestures between us with her finger—"is not my proposal. You will propose one day, when we are both ready for it, and you will make it good. Do you hear me? Good. The words 'I wasn't, actually, but I can,' will not come out of your mouth at that time. Understood?"

"Yes, ma'am."

"Good." She narrows her eyes at me as if she's not sure if my yes was sincere or not.

"Can I say something?"

"What?" she snaps.

"This bossy girl thing is a real turn-on."

A slow smile spread across her face at that along with the hint of a blush.

"Can I say something else?"

"Okay," she agrees, this time smiling.

"You were right when you said you've been doing all the work and I want to fix that. Will you let me? Because I really need to earn that seven percent back."

"Hmm." She hums while she thinks. "I do have a few badges left to earn. Perhaps you could help me with them."

"I'd love to."

EPILOGUE

"ONCE UPON A TIME a girl walked into a bar and captured my heart, but I was too stupid to see what was happening. Luckily for me she was a very goal-oriented type of girl who decided against all logic that I was goal-worthy. I wasn't, but that didn't stop her. Thank God that didn't stop her."

"Rhys!" Lydia hisses. "Don't tell him that! That is not an accurate retelling of the fairytale. Nor an appropriate retelling."

"Hush. It's our favorite bedtime story. Also he's a dog so I don't think he minds which version I give him."

We both turn to look at our new dog, Trooper. He thumps his tail against the floor and tilts his head to the side, one eye raised as he attempts to discern if Lydia is about to give him an extra belly rub before bed. He's some kind of lab mix we obtained through a rescue group, but I don't think that should be a surprise to anyone. Lydia loves to rescue things. People, old sheets, lost tourists, a pair of swans that

265

needed a sponsorship—honestly I didn't ask for the details on that last one. Trooper's an adult dog and badly behaved. Much like I was when Lydia found me. She says he has potential.

"Does he have to sleep in his kennel?"

Trooper thumps his tail in response. He knows how to work me.

"Yes. Yes, he does. Until he's earned his good behavior badge he needs to sleep in his crate."

"He's only eaten two of your shoes," I point out. Trooper hangs his head and emits a dramatic grunt. "And one was a flip flop. That hardly counts."

"It counts, Rhys. So does eating half a pound of ground beef off the counter after he distracted me by overturning his water bowl."

Trooper rolls onto his back and thumps his tail again.

"What if the best dog he can be is still awful?" I reach over and give him a belly rub.

"Then I'll get new shoes."

"Or you could just run around barefoot and pregnant, rendering the shoes irrelevant."

"You'd like me barefoot and pregnant? That sounds horribly inconvenient."

"Which? Being barefoot or being pregnant?"

"Barefoot while pregnant. Imagine you cut your foot while barefoot but you were so pregnant you couldn't reach your own foot to take care of it."

"Lydia." I stand and motion for Trooper to get into his kennel. He does so without complaint, turning in a circle before settling with his head on his front paws.

"What?"

"I think we should talk about doing the reproductive kind of mating. Have some cygnets of our own."

Lydia beams. "You know that baby swans are called cygnets?"

"Of course I do." Fine. I paid a little bit of attention to the swan sponsorship packet.

"Babe. That is so sexy." Lydia's eyeing me and licking her lips like she does when I return from the gym, shirt off and slung over my shoulder.

She's still too easy.

"We could buy a house. Trooper needs a yard. The kids will need a yard. And I could be wrong, but I'm almost positive that no school bus is going to make a pickup on the Strip."

"We could buy a fixer-upper!" Lydia exclaims. She's moved to the bed and she's sitting cross-legged on the surface, wearing a pair of sheet pajama pants and a tank top.

"Or we could build," I offer. "Find the perfect lot with a view of the Strip on one side and mountains on the other. Custom build."

"Or we could buy a fixer-upper!"

"Or we could buy a fixer-upper," I agree. Because once I get my head out of my ass I'm not that much of an idiot.

"It'll be just like an episode of *House Hunters*," Lydia says dreamily. "Only I'll get to look at all the houses instead of just three."

"It'll be just like that," I agree. "Only better."

I've spent every day since I thought I'd blown it with her appreciating her. Appreciating what we have together. We've spent weekends exploring Vegas. Weekends traveling. Evenings doing nothing and days doing everything. We've been to Austin for the taco trucks and San Antonio for the puffy tacos. When we went to Paris for our honeymoon we had crêpes and she called them French tacos. Then she laughed at herself until she nearly fell over. I fell in love with her all over again.

Lydia makes every experience better. Being with her feels like luck and fate and winning the lottery. It feels like trust and friendship and home. Her love feels like a surprise so good you'd never dare expect it, but when it finds you, you hold on tight.

And I will. I'll hang onto my good girl forever.

GOOD TIME

(PAYTON & VINCE)

Coming Fall 2018

There's one thing you should know.
I wasn't *that* drunk.

I was more than sober enough to put a stop to it. The truth is, it was my idea. I'm the one who suggested it.

I knew it was crazy, but it's not as if I'd be the first girl to get married on a whim in Las Vegas. I wouldn't even be the last girl to get married on a whim in Las Vegas.

So what's my excuse? I liked him. I liked the idea that he'd be stuck with me, just for a little bit.

Because nothing good ever lasts, so you might as well have a good time while you can.

GOOD TIME

Add it to Goodreads!

ACKNOWLEDGMENTS

This one took a village... of people talking me off the ledge.

Liv Morris,
Thank you for telling the cutest story about your daughter kissing a man in a bar and telling me I could have it because it would be weird if you used material from your own daughter. ☺ Readers please note: real life Lydia kissed the bartender. She did not do any of the crazy things fictional Lydia did.

Kayti McGee,
Thank you for thinking this book is the funniest thing ever and sending me voice messages that were sometimes indiscernible through your laughter but were always a huge boost to my fragile snowflake confidence. You are the best & your support was invaluable!

Staci Hart,
Thank you for the late-night messages in which we exchanged a nonstop rotation of:
"My book sucks!"
"My book is so good. Holy crap."
"It's official. This is the worst thing I've ever

written."
"I fixed everything and I think it's going to be okay!"
"My book sucks so bad man. I think I need to get a new job."
"This book is my favorite of all the books!"

Raine Miller, Amy Daws, Sierra Simone, Laurelin Paige, CD Reiss, Jade West,
Thank you for your friendship.

Lauren Lascola-Lesczynski,
Thank you for your friendship & support and for making me laugh so hard I peed my pants.
I appreciate you & your friendship so hard!

Candi Kane, Sarah Piechuta,
Thank you for all your help and support with this release. I cannot thank you enough for helping me ease the workload.

Letitia Hasser, Kari March,
Thank you for for the cover & graphics!

Jean Siska, Melissa Gaston, Beverly Gardner Tubb, Mila Tracey, Melissa Panio-Peterson,
Thank you for being early readers & reading when it was unfinished and messy and still wanting more. You have no idea how much this means.

ABOUT THE AUTHOR

Jana Aston likes cats, big coffee cups and books about billionaires who deflower virgins. She wrote her debut novel while fielding customer service calls about electrical bills, and she's ever grateful for the fictional gynecologist in Wrong that readers embraced so much she was able to make working in her pajamas a reality.

Jana's novels have appeared on the NYT, USA Today and Wall Street Journal bestsellers list, some multiple times. She likes multiples.

SOCIAL MEDIA

I have a reader group on Facebook & I'd love to see you there! If you're into that sort of thing, please join us in the Grind Me Café:
bit.ly/GrindMeCafe

Facebook page Jana Aston
bit.ly/FBJanaAston

Twitter @janaaston
bit.ly/TwitterJanaAston

Instagram JanaAston
bit.ly/IGJanaAston

Website
www.janaaston.com

Signed Paperbacks
bit.ly/SignedJana

If you prefer to avoid social media & have my release news sent straight to your mailbox, sign up for my newsletter here:
bit.ly/NewsletterJana

ALSO BY JANA ASTON

Wrong
Right
Fling
Trust

Times Square
Sure Thing

Printed in Great Britain
by Amazon